# The Case of the
# Missing Fan Dancer

## John Bekker Mystery Series

Sunset

Sunrise

First Light

This Side of Midnight

With Six You Get Wally

Who Killed Joe Italiano?

For Better or Worse

## Other books by Nero Award-winning author Al Lamanda

Dunston Falls

Walking Homeless

Running Homeless

City of Darkness

Once Upon a Time on 9/11

# The Case of the Missing Fan Dancer

A John Bekker Mystery

# Al Lamanda

Encircle Publications
Farmington, Maine, U.S.A.

Cover design by Christopher Wait
Cover photograph © Getty Images

Published by:

Encircle Publications
PO Box 187
Farmington, ME 04938

info@encirclepub.com
http://encirclepub.com

# Chapter One

I was at the trailer at the beach, packing up files. Today would be the last time I would be able to claim the trailer and tiny bit of beach as my own.

Forty plus years ago, a local real estate developer had the idea of creating a trailer park on a deserted stretch of beach for surfers. At one time there were twenty-four trailer for rent or purchase, a surfing store, an ice cream and snack stand and a full time instructor.

By the time I came along, just two trailers remained, the one I occupied and the one belonging to Oz.

Prior to my downward spire into a whiskey bottle where I lived for a decade, I was a police sergeant in charge of special crimes. I got too close to organized crime and needed to be taught a lesson.

They came for me. They got my wife instead. Our five-year-old daughter Regan had the misfortune of watching her mother being murdered. Regan spent a decade in a hospital for traumatized children. I spent the like amount of time living inside a bottle.

I lost my job, the house, everything.

Homelessness had spared me when my sister-in-law Janet, found the vacant trailer on the beach near Oz's and we drank away the days and nights for ten years.

I've been sober for three years now. Much has happened since. I was hired by the very mobster I believed responsible for my wife's murder to find the man who actually killed her. I have a private investigator's license, a pension from the PD, a home not far from the ocean, my daughter living with me, a dog and a cat and Oz.

And County Sheriff Jane Morgan, who might or might not become the second Mrs. Bekker, depending upon her mood.

Regan came out of the trailer with a box of files and set it on the card table next to my chair.

"This is the last one," she said.

"Thanks, honey," I said.

It was hard for me to believe Regan would turn twenty in a few months. Depending on who you ask, you'll get a different answer as to what is the most valuable commodity.

Some say gold, others say health, others say money and still others say land and property.

They are all wrong.

The most valuable commodity is time.

Just ask the billionaire who is on his deathbed what he would pay for more time.

It came to mind looking at Regan. She's a bit of a thing, with dark hair and her mother's features and I missed ten years of her life I will never get back.

Time.

The most valuable commodity.

"So today is it, huh?' Regan said.

What happened was, another developer came along and convinced the county this deserted stretch of beach would be an ideal location for beachfront condos. The county invoked eminent domain laws and Oz and I could take the forty thousand dollars offered us for the trailer, or we could stay put and be forced out without a penny.

We took the money, met with the developer and plunked down the eighty thousand on a three-bedroom condo facing the ocean.

It would make a nice weekend getaway. As soon as plans and blueprints are ready, we'll pick out our unit.

"The condos will go up in no time," I said.

"Let's go out with a bang," Regan said. "One last cookout before they haul it away."

"Got your cell phone?" I said.

Regan whipped it out of her back packet.

"Call your Uncle Walt, Oz and Jane," I said.

"The ladies?"

Regan always referred to Carly Simms and Campbell Crist as the ladies.

"Sure, why not," I said.

Regan went inside the trailer to make the calls. I opened the lid on the box of files and rifled through old case logs and notes.

Twenty minutes later, Regan emerged and set a fresh cup of coffee on the card table.

"Oz said should he bring Molly and Cuddles. I told him yes," Regan said. "Uncle Walt said what time. Jane said should she bring anything. Campbell said she'd rather walk barefoot over hot coals, but Carly said they'd be here."

"There is only one thing left to do," I said. "Take a last run on the beach and then hit the grocery store."

"That's two things," Regan said. "And I kind of like the second better than the first."

"No allowance for you this week," I said.

"I have a job, remember? I don't get an allowance."

"Get changed," I said.

Regan worked three times a week at a pet store in town. She didn't need to, but it was good therapy for her to mix with people. She had a trust fund left to her by mobster Eddie Crist, which she had yet to touch.

She emerged from the trailer wearing sweats and running shoes.

I went in and tossed on shorts, a tee-shirt and running shoes. Then we walked close to the water's edge.

"Remember I'm five-one, not six-four," Regan said.

"Six miles?" I said.

"Three," Regan said.

"Four?"

"Three and a half and not a step more."

"Sold."

We started slowly to warm up. After a half mile, I opened it up a bit. Regan kept pace. We reached the two-mile mark and turned around. I opened it up a bit more and again Regan kept pace.

We closed it out with a burst to the finish line where Regan proceeded to flop on her back, gasp for air and look up at me.

"Monster," she said. "That was four."

"Let's change and hit the store," I said.

\* \* \*

I added a few logs to the trashcan to keep the fire going. Days are warm and nights are cool at the beach this time of year.

Walt and his wife Elizabeth were to my right. Jane and Regan to my left. Oz, Campbell and Carly were opposite me.

Campbell and Carly's nine-month-old baby girl was asleep in her carrier between them. Carly gently rocked the carrier.

Molly, our cat was asleep on Regan's lap. Cuddles, our fifteen-pound pug, slept between Jane and Regan.

Regan and I picked up burgers, hot dogs, steak tips, chicken tenders for the grill and baked beans and baked potatoes that Regan prepared inside.

There wasn't much left except for the belching.

"Gonna miss this place," Oz said.

"We'll be back when the condo's are built," I said.

"Who wants coffee?" Regan said.

Only everybody and Regan went inside to make a full pot.

"Now that I'm reinstated, I'm thinking of retirement," Walt said.

"About time," Elizabeth said. "All those missed vacations."

"What vacations?" Walt said.

"The ones we never took," Elizabeth said.

"What about you, Jane?" Walt said.

"Toying with the idea," Jane said. "Twenty-five years in and counting might just be enough."

"You'd finally be able to do something with your hair," Campbell said.

"You said you'd be nice," Carly said.

"What?" Campbell said.

"Hey, take it from an old man," Oz said. "Don't be in big hurry to grow old. Being old is no picnic."

Time.

The most valuable commodity.

# Chapter Two

The sunrise over the ocean is a sight I never tire of.

Regan and I sat in our chairs and watched the magic of the sun rise over the ocean for the last time from this particular point of view.

"I better check to make sure we didn't forget anything," I said.

I went inside the trailer and checked the two bedrooms, living room, kitchen and bathroom. When I returned outside, Regan was standing up, squinting into the sun.

"What?" I said.

"Someone's coming."

I squinted into the sun. A lone figure was running toward us about three hundred yards out. Well, not exactly running. More like… I don't know what to call it.

"Dad, I think it's Wally," Regan said.

The figure fell down, flopped around for a bit and slowly stood up.

"It is Wally," I said.

"What's he doing?"

"Running. Sort of," I said.

As Wally came closer, he screamed, "Mr. Bekker, it's me, Wally," and then fell over again.

"Oh for," Regan said. "Dad, he's going to kill himself."

"Wally, slow down," I yelled.

He slowed to a walk until he reached us.

"Mr. Bekker," he said, collapsed to all fours and then threw up.

"Jesus, Wally," Regan said.

"Sorry," Wally gasped.

I helped him to a chair. "What are you doing here?" I said.

Wally is Wally Sample, one of the six owners of the Sample Iced Tea Corporation. His family disowned him because they thought he was an insane, degenerate gambler, but in reality he's a quirky genius. He runs logistics for the entire company and has brought the company to soaring profits.

"Take your time, Wally," I said. "And tell me why you're here."

"Bubbles," Wally said.

"What?" I said.

"I think he said bubbles," Regan said.

"They took her," Wally said. "They took my Bubbles."

"Who took what?" I said.

"Bubbles, Dad. Didn't you hear?" Regan said.

"I… Wally, who is Bubbles?" I said.

"My fiancé," Wally said.

"Your what?" I said.

"His fiancé, Dad," Regan said.

"Regan, bring us all some coffee," I said.

She went inside the trailer for the coffee.

"Now Wally, who is Bubbles?" I said.

"Barbara Bouchette," Wally said.

Regan returned with three mugs of coffee. "Why do you call her Bubbles?" she said.

"Oh, well, see, before she agreed to marry me that was her stripper name," Wally said. "She does this thing with balloons."

"Oh boy," Regan said.

"Maybe you should start at the beginning," I said.

"Oh, well, see, what happened was one of our warehouse

7

executives got married and his friends threw him a bachelor party," Wally said. "I was asked to go and I went. They hired a stripper."

"Bubbles," Regan said.

"That's right. How did you know?" Wally said.

"You just said she was a… never mind," Regan said.

"Continue," I said.

"Well when she came out of that giant cake, it was love at first sight," Wally said.

Regan rolled her eyes.

Now Wally stands about five-foot-three and is shaped like a pear, His hair is a mess, as is his clothes and sometimes he wears two different color shoes.

"So you met at the bachelor party?" I said.

"And we been together ever since," Wally said. "Oh, wait."

Wally dropped to his knees and scratched a long, complicated math equation in the sand. Regan and I watched him until, satisfied, he stood up.

"I've been working on that for weeks," Wally said.

Looking at the equation, Regan said, "What is it?"

"Oh, well, see it's the—" Wally said.

"Never mind that now," I said. "What happened to Bubbles?"

"I rented her an apartment in White Plains until we get married," Wally said. "Last night, I went over to see her and she was gone and there was the note."

"What note?" I said.

"The ransom note."

"Do you have it?" I said.

"Yes."

I waited. Regan rolled her eyes again.

"May I see it?" I said.

"What? Oh, yes, of course," Wally said.

He patted his jacket pockets and then dug a rolled up into a ball piece of paper and handed it to me. I unraveled the ball and looked at the typed note.

*If you want to see Bubbles alive again, the price is 15 million. No police or FBI or it won't end well for her. Await the next set of instructions by phone in 48 hours.*

"It was on the coffee table," Wally said.

"Did you call the police?" I said.

"I got on the company jet and flew here to see you," Wally said. "And my family wasn't too happy about that."

"Do you have 15 million?" I said.

"I can get it," Wally said.

"When did you get the note?" I said.

"About eight last night," Wally said.

"Twelve hours ago," I said. "So you have thirty-six hours before the call."

"You have to help me, Mr. Bekker," Wally said. "That's why I brought the jet, to bring you back with me."

"Oh boy," Regan said.

# Chapter Three

Walt examined the ransom note and shook his head. "Care to make bets the only prints on it are yours and Wally's," he said.

"I know that," I said. "Can your tech people identify the type, see if they can name the printer?"

"Sure, in about a month," Walt said. "Jack, kidnapping is FBI, you know that."

"I already called Pail Lawrence," I said.

"Like one of the FBI bigwigs doesn't have anything better to do," Walt said.

"The Sample family is one of the wealthiest and well known families in the country," I said. "He'll take charge."

"Yeah, he might at that," Walt said.

"He should be calling me here pretty soon," I said.

We were in the living room of my house.

"Where is old Wally?" Walt said.

"In the yard with Regan and Oz," I said.

"Let's have a word with him," Walt said.

We went to the kitchen where I opened the sliding door and we stepped out to the backyard. Regan, Oz and Wally were at the picnic table. Wally was eating a chocolate donut.

"Hello, Wally," Walt said.

"Hello Captain Grimes," Wally said.

"Wally, I'd like to… Regan, anymore of those donuts?" Walt said.

"I'll get coffee and donuts for everybody," Regan said.

She went inside, followed by Cuddles.

"Wally, do you have 15 million dollars?" Walt said.

"We made two billion in sales last year," Wally said. "I think we can spare it for my beautiful Bubbles."

"Tell me about… Bubbles," Walt said.

"She's beautiful and sweet," Wally said.

"And a stripper," Walt said.

"No, see, only part time to pay for her college tuition," Wally said. "After she agreed to marry me she quit."

"Do you have a photo of her?" I said.

Wally dug out his wallet and produced a photo of him and Bubbles. She was a striking brunette and a good six inches taller than Wally.

"Where was this taken?" I said.

"At the amusement park in Rye about a month ago," Wally said.

"Tall girl," Walt said.

"It doesn't bother her," Wally said. "Or me either. Mr. Bekker, she just has to be alright. I don't know what I'd do if—"

"Don't get ahead of yourself," I said.

Regan returned with a tray of coffee and donuts.

"Have a donut," I said.

"Who can eat," Wally said as he grabbed a donut.

The hard line phone inside rang. "I'll get it," I said.

I went to the kitchen and grabbed the wall phone. "Jack, Paul," Lawrence said.

"What's the verdict?" I said.

"I'm flying into White Plains airport at two this afternoon," Lawrence said. "I'll be there by four."

"Grab a cab to the Sample home office, we'll meet you there."

"See you there," Lawrence said.

11

I hung up and returned to the backyard.

"Wally, is your jet standing by?" I said.

"At the airport."

"Call the pilot and tell him we'll be there in an hour," I said.

"You're going to New York?" Regan said.

"As soon as I pack a bag," I said.

Oz looked at me.

"Take care of things for a few days," I said.

Oz nodded. "We be fine," he said.

"Wally?" I said.

"Yes?"

"Your pilot, call him," I said.

Wally licked chocolate cream off his fingers and took out his cell phone.

*　*　*

The Sample corporate jet held a dozen people. It was just Wally and I on board.

As the pilot taxied us to the runway of the private airfield, Wally gripped his seat armrests and closed his eyes. "I hate flying," he said. "Hate it."

"Just relax, Wally," I said.

As the jet gained speed for liftoff, Wally said, "Hate it, hate it, hate it."

We took off as smooth as silk but Wally gripped the armrests to tightly his knuckles turned white.

The jet turned and gained in altitude and finally Wally opened his eyes. "The take off and landing is the most dangerous part of flying," he said.

"Try to relax now," I said. "Tell me about Bubbles."

"Mr. Bekker, she's wonderful," Wally said. "She bright and funny and doesn't care how short I am or what other people think. She loves me the way that I am."

"I'm sure she does," I said.

"I know what everybody thinks," Wally said. "She's after the money. My family said she's making a fool of me. Even if she was, I don't care. I love her and she makes me happy."

The seatbelt sign went out and I unbuckled mine. "How about something to drink?" I said.

"I could use a little nosh," Wally said.

"Sure."

The fridge in the galley was filled with various flavors of Sample Iced Tea. The freezer was packed with frozen foods of every type. I put on a small pot of coffee and then nuked waffles.

We ate waffles with iced tea and watched a game show on the flat screen television mounted on the wall.

It was one of those brainiac game shows where each question was harder than the previous and Wally rambled off every answer correctly without pausing to think first.

After the game show ended, I had some coffee and said, "Wally, what about her family? Have you met them?"

"Not yet," Wally said. "We had plans to go to Pittsburgh, where she's from so I could meet them."

"I see," I said. "Have you met her friends?"

"She didn't have many," Wally said. "Between taking classes and working, she didn't have many."

"Okay, that's enough for now," I said. "Let's watch another game show."

After another show, the seatbelt sign came on and the pilot told us we would be landing in fifteen minutes.

Wally tensed up, gripped the arm rests and as the jet descended, he said, "Here we go, here we go," and he didn't open his eyes until we were on the ground.

# Chapter Four

A driver for Sample Iced Tea met us at the private airport in White Plains and drove us to the headquarters building on Main Street.

White Plains is a wealthy corporate town about forty miles north of Manhattan. It's home to a dozen large companies, including Sample Iced Tea.

Paul Lawrence was waiting for us in the large, posh lobby of the Sample Iced Tea building.

"Jack," he said.

"Paul, this is Wally Sample," I said. "Wally, Paul Lawrence from the FBI. He's an old friend and he helped me last year with your problem."

"Hello," Wally said.

"First, is there someplace we can talk?" Lawrence said.

"My office," Wally said.

\* \* \*

If you could empty the contents of Wally's brain, it would look like his office. Cluttered.

Paper, stacks of reports, stuff every and anywhere. To an outsider it would appear to be total chaos. To Wally it all made perfect sense.

Wally plopped into the chair behind his desk.

I removed piles of papers and a shit from a chair and Lawrence dug a chair out from under a mountain of files and we sat.

"Wally, may I see the ransom note," Lawrence said.

Wally removed it from a pocket and handed it to Lawrence. Lawrence looked at me.

"It was rolled in a ball," I said.

Lawrence nodded and read the note. "We have about twenty-nine hours to work with," he said.

"You mean find her?" Wally said.

"To find who kidnapped her," Lawrence said.

"I don't… wait, do you think they killed her?" Wally said.

"I won't lie to you Wally, the odds are against her being found alive," Lawrence said.

"When they call, I'll demand to talk to her," Wally said.

"Can you get 15 million dollars?" Lawrence said.

"We need to see my brother Bob," Wally said.

*   *   *

The family had assembled in the boardroom.

Robert Sample Jr. was the oldest of the six Sample heirs and the company CEO. Steven was next in line and the VP of Operations. Susan was VP of Product Control. Amy was VP of marketing. Barbara was VP of Finance.

The five of them stared at us as we sat at the boardroom table.

"Before we start, let me go on record as saying there is no fucking way I am cutting a check for my imbecilic brother's whore," Barbara said.

"She's a stripper, not a whore," Wally said.

"Explain to me the difference," Barbara said.

"Barbara, please," Robert said. "Let's hear what Mr. Lawrence has to say."

"The FBI can't force you to pay the ransom," Lawrence said.

"Good, cause we're not," Barbara said.

"Barbara, let Mr. Lawrence speak, please," Robert said.

"I can't guarantee you Miss Bouchette is even alive," Lawrence said. "But I urge you to make every attempt to cooperate with the kidnappers."

Barbara tapped her foot under the desk. "You mean pay the fifteen million is what you mean," she said.

"The FBI will do everything in its power to return Miss Bouchette alive and the money to you intact," Lawrence said.

Barbara glared at Wally. "Fifteen million for this whore, Wally. Does she have gold between her legs?"

"That's enough, Barbara," Robert said. "Despite what you think, Wally has been brilliant with logistics and has saved us millions in cost overhead."

"If this woman makes Wally happy, who are we to judge?" Susan said. "I vote to pay the ransom."

"I do too," Amy said.

"As do I," Steven said.

"Robert?" Barbara said.

Robert nodded.

"Well, that's just fucking great," Barbara said. "Has it occurred to you that if they get away with this so easily any one of us could be next?"

"Statistics prove a kidnapper never strikes in the same place twice," Lawrence said. "They may use the same MO, but never in the same place."

"Tell that to the Lindbergh baby," Barbara said.

"Oh for God's sake, Barbara," Robert said.

"The FBI will investigate this incident with or without the money," Lawrence said. "With the money increases the chances of finding Miss Bouchette alive."

16

"Barbara, get the money to the FBI," Robert said.

"Thank you, Mr. Sample," Lawrence said. "If you could have it tomorrow morning. Right now we have a great deal of work to do."

"Next time, Wally, keep it in your pants," Barbara said.

"That's enough, Barbara," Robert said.

"We'll be in touch in the morning," Lawrence said.

\*   \*   \*

We stood in front of the lobby doors after leaving the board room.

"Wally, where is your car?" Lawrence said.

"I don't own one," Wally said. "Or maybe I do, I forget."

"We'll take a cab then," Lawrence said. "I'll call Uber if you give me your address."

"My address?" Wally said.

"Yes, where you live," Lawrence said.

"I just usually have a driver take me home," Wally said. "He knows the way."

Lawrence looked at me. "He grows on you," I said.

# Chapter Five

Wally had a large condo about a mile from the headquarters building. Like his office, the place was a disaster. Papers, notebooks, file folders and dirty clothes were piled high everywhere.

"I'd like to have the Manhattan lab boys meet us at Miss Bouchette's apartment," Lawrence said.

"Okay," Wally said.

Lawrence looked at Wally and waited.

"Wally, I think Paul wants you to take us there," I said.

"Oh, I better tell the driver," Wally said.

The apartment Wally rented for Barbara Bouchette was actually a sublet if a condo in Main Street.

The condo was on the fourth floor. The building was nice, real nice with a backyard courtyard garden.

"All this furniture?" Lawrence said.

Wally looked at the furniture.

"Paul means did it come furnished," I said.

"Oh, yes, it did," Wally said. "The furniture I mean."

Lawrence put on latex gloves and gave me a pair. We walked from room-to-room, checking the closets and bathroom.

"Wally, are these her clothes?" Lawrence said

"Yes, and her shoes," Wally said.

"The items in the bathroom, hers?" Lawrence said.

Wally nodded.

The FBI lab technicians arrived and Lawrence let them in.

"Dust everything for prints and see if you can find DNA in the bathroom," Lawrence said. "And take this ransom note to the lab and see if you can identify the brand of printer."

A technician took the rumpled note and looked at Lawrence, who shrugged.

Lawrence looked at his watch. "Twenty-two hours before the call," he said. "How many bedrooms at your condo?" he said to Wally.

"Two, but the sofa is one of those pullout beds," Wally said. "The third bedroom I use as a den."

"Jack, flip a coin for the daybed," Lawrence said.

*   *   *

We ordered Chinese food for dinner and ate at Wally's kitchen table, after he dumped the clutter on it to the floor.

"Wally, how are you feeling?" Lawrence said.

"Sick, worried, stressed, my stomach is upset and I have a headache," Wally said. "And my feet hurt."

"I think Paul means are you up for some questions?" I said.

"Oh, umm, sure. I guess."

"Good," Lawrence said. "Now tell me everything you know about Miss Bouchette."

"When you say everything, what exactly do you mean?" Wally said.

"How you met, what does she do besides jumping out of cakes, where did she go to college, like that," I said.

"Oh, well, see, we met at the bachelor party they had at the warehouse for the foreman," Wally said. "I oversee logistics for the warehouses, so I was invited. I didn't plan to stay long, but when Bubbles popped out of the cake, I couldn't help myself. She was so beautiful."

"I need a photo of her for identification purposes," Lawrence said.

Wally nodded.

"So you met her at the bachelor party and what happened next?" Lawrence said.

"We just hit it off," Wally said. "And I know what you're thinking. Money. Well, she wasn't like that. She worked as a stripper to pay her tuition at The College of Westchester where she studies business. She is very smart."

"I'm sure she is," Lawrence said.

"She was a good cook and would make dinner for me three or four times a week," Wally said.

"Where is she from?" Lawrence said.

"Pittsburgh, like I told Mr. Bekker," Wally said.

"Did she have a car?"

"No. She rode the bus or walked."

"But she did have a driver's license?" Lawrence said.

"I… don't know. I never asked. What does that have to do with anything?"

"Probably nothing," Lawrence said. "But what I'm wondering is how anyone knew she was your girlfriend. Somebody knew you're a Sample and worth a great deal of money."

"Maybe somebody saw us at a restaurant or something?" Wally said.

"Possibly," Lawrence said.

"Did she have a lot of friends?" Lawrence said.

"Some of the girls who worked with," Wally said. "She would talk to some of them on the phone. I heard her tell one of them she was quitting her stripper job."

"What was the name of the company she worked for?" Lawrence said.

"I don't know, I didn't hire her," Wally said.

"That's alright," Lawrence said. "We'll find out."

"I'm tired," Wally said. "Can I go to bed?"

"Sure," Lawrence said.

Wally sat there and stared into space for a few moments.

Lawrence looked at me.

"Wally?" I said.

Wally jumped to his feet, looked around, grabbed a notebook off the floor, grabbed a pen off the table, sat and proceeded to scribble on a page.

After about a minute of scribbling, Wally closed the notebook, stood up and said, "Well, goodnight," and walked to his bedroom.

"Jesus Christ, Jack," Lawrence said.

"I know," I said.

"I've seen setups before, but this one takes the stripper's cake," Lawrence said.

"It's possible it's a legit kidnapping," I said.

"And it's possible I will be voted sexiest man alive, too," Lawrence said.

"But you're going to treat it as such," I said.

"You know better than that," Lawrence said.

"See you in the morning," I said.

"Enjoy the sofa," Lawrence said.

# Chapter Six

In the morning, after I made coffee, I rummaged through the kitchen.

"Wally, do you realize the only thing you have for breakfast is Froot Loops?" I said when Wally stumbled into the kitchen.

"I like Froot Loops. Where is Mr. Lawrence?" Wally said.

"In the living room on the phone," I said.

I filled a cup with coffee and set it on the table. "Sit, I want to talk to you," I said.

Wally sat and took a sip of coffee.

I filled a cup for myself and sat opposite Wally.

"Wally, when was the last time you saw Miss Bouchette?" I said.

"The night before I found the note," Wally said. "We went to dinner at the Italian place on Central Avenue. Then we went to her condo and then I went home."

"And the next day?"

"She was supposed to meet me for breakfast," Wally said. "The driver took me to her condo. When she didn't come down, I rang the bell. She didn't answer, so I used my key and went in and found the note."

Lawrence entered the kitchen. "Let's get some breakfast before we go to the office," he said.

"Don't you like Froot Loops?" I said.

* * *

The driver took us to a large diner on Central Avenue.

I ordered scrambled eggs with bacon and hash browns. As did Lawrence. Wally ordered pancakes, fried eggs, sausages, bacon, a blueberry muffin and prunes and a vanilla milkshake.

"My family isn't happy with me," Wally said.

"Nobody is ever happy about a kidnapping," Lawrence said.

"No, see, they..." Wally said, paused, grabbed napkin and scribbled a note.

Lawrence sighed.

Wally tucked the napkin into his shirt pocket.

"Wally?" Lawrence said.

"Yes," Wally said.

"You were saying?" Lawrence said.

"I was saying what?" Wally said.

"Never mind," Lawrence said.

* * *

Robert said, "Barbara and two of our security people are at the bank right now, withdrawing the funds."

"Thank you," Wally said.

"Six FBI Agents will be here in about an hour to record the serial numbers on the bills," Lawrence said.

"Will the bills be marked?" Robert said.

"That's the first thing they will look for," Lawrence said. "If they find any markings, Miss Bouchette is guaranteed to be killed."

"The odds of them doing that anyway?" Robert said.

"If they get what they want, they will probably let her go," Lawrence said. "They know we won't give up looking for them and kidnapping and extortion are bad enough, why add murder to the charges?"

"I see," Robert said.

"Your brother, is he always so…?" Lawrence said.

"Always," Robert said. "By the way, where is he?"

"We left him in his office," I said.

"Call me when the money arrives," Lawrence said.

\* \* \*

Wally wasn't in his office. We found him in the company cafeteria eating waffles.

Lawrence and I grabbed cups of coffee and joined him at his table.

"Didn't we just have breakfast?" Lawrence said.

"I eat when I'm stressed," Wally said.

"Your family came through with the money," I said.

"Thank God," Wally said.

"I have a team of agents arriving shortly to record the bills," Lawrence said. "Jack, why don't you take Wally home and I'll join you there later."

\* \* \*

I changed out of my suit and into jeans and shirt and found Wally in the kitchen, eating a bowl of Froot Loops.

"Wally, your stomach is going to burst," I said.

"She's dead, isn't she?" Wally said.

"You don't know that," I said.

"Look at me, Mr. Bekker," Wally said. "I know what I am. I'm a clumsy little buffoon and I know it. The family doesn't want me and neither did anyone else. Bubbles made me feel loved. Like I mattered. Does it matter if she was a stripper? Does it matter if all she wanted was money? Not to me it didn't. And now she's gone."

"Wally, listen," I said. "These people are smart enough to know the FBI won't stop looking for them. Why add murder to kidnapping and extortion?"

"So there's a chance?" Wally said.

I nodded. "There's a chance."

"I'm going to take a nap so I'll be awake for tonight," Wally said.

After Wally went to his bedroom, I used my cell phone to call home.

"Hey, Dad," Regan said. "How's Wally?"

"Wally is Wally," I said. "What are you guys up to?"

"I'm going to work at the pet store and Oz is walking Buddy. When are you coming home?"

"Couple of days."

"Dad, be careful," Regan said.

"I'm in the background," I said. "The FBI is handling things."

"Good," Regan said. "Want me to tell Oz to call you?"

"I'll call later," I said. "Have a nice day at work."

After I hung up with Regan, I called Jane.

"Where are you?" she said. "I called your hard line and Regan said you went to White Plains with Wally."

"His girlfriend was kidnapped," I said.

"Wally has a girlfriend?" Jane said.

"Her name is Bubbles," I said.

"She's a stripper," Jane said.

"Strippers are people too, you know," I said.

"Hey, at one time I thought about doing it myself," Jane said.

"If you had, you'd get my last dollar," I said.

"You sweet talker you," Jane said. "So seriously, she's been kidnapped?"

"Ransom is 15 million. I have Paul Lawrence with me now," I said.

"Jesus," Jane said. "When you coming home?"

"Few days."

"I'll keep the bed warm for you."

After hanging up with Jane, I pulled out the sofa bed and took a nap.

# Chapter Seven

Wally ate spare ribs while we waited for the phone to ring. Lawrence and I drank coffee.

Six FBI agents sat around the living room with recording and tracing equipment.

I was wondering why I quit smoking.

The phone rang. Agents sprang into action. Lawrence nodded to Wally and he answered the landline phone in the kitchen.

Wally listened carefully for a few seconds and then said, "I don't really need a food chopper, but thanks for calling."

"A telemarketer?" Lawrence said. "Hang up."

Wally hung up and returned to his ribs.

I made a fresh pot of coffee and passed out cups.

The phone rang again. Wally got up again. The agents activated their equipment again. Lawrence and I listened to the call on the equipment in the living room.

"Hello," Wally said/

"Did you get the money?" A deep voice said.

"I got it," Wally said.

"Good. Convert it to bearer bonds. You have twenty-four hours and I'll—"

"What are bearer bonds?" Wally said.

"What?" the deep voice said.

"I don't know what they are," Wally said.

"They're… have your people explain it to you. Jesus Christ," the deep voice said. "I will call back in twenty-four hours with instructions."

"Wait," Wally said as the phone went dead.

"That's a new one," Lawrence said.

"What are bearer bonds?" Wally said.

"Government bonds that say pay to the bearer," I said. "No records are kept of them."

"Play back the call," Lawrence said.

We listened to the call a half dozen times.

"See if you can get a voice print on him," Lawrence said.

Even using a voice scrambler, a voice print was possible. Remote, but possible.

"Wally, call your brother," I said. "Robert."

"Okay. Wait. I don't know his number," Wally said.

"Is your driver still on duty?" I said.

"Mr. Lawrence told him to wait," Wally said.

\* \* \*

Robert Sample lived in a large house about a mile or so from Wally. He saw us in his study away from his family.

"I take it there was a problem with the call," Robert said.

"He wants the ransom in bearer bonds," Lawrence said.

"Untraceable and unregistered," Robert said. "Pretty smart."

"What is your main bank?" Lawrence said.

"Bank of Manhattan. It's a private, commercial bank."

"Tomorrow morning, the three of us will visit the Bank of Manhattan and convert the cash to bonds," Lawrence said.

"They open at nine," Robert said. "I'll have you picked up at seven-thirty."

\* \* \*

Wally was alone in his condo when we returned.

"They said to tell you they went to the lab," Wally said.

"We'll get the bonds in the morning," I said.

"Feel like some dinner?" Lawrence said.

"I'll go with you, but I can't eat," Wally said.

I asked the driver if he knew any Italian restaurants in the area and he took us to one near the Trump Tower at City Center.

I ordered the veal Parmesan. Lawrence went with the chicken Parmesan. Wally ordered one of each and a side order of meatballs and garlic bread.

"I thought you weren't hungry?" Lawrence said.

"Eating relaxes me," Wally said.

"Wally, who got married?" I said.

Wally looked at me. "Is that like a knock-knock joke?" he said.

"At your warehouse where you met Bubbles," I said.

"Oh, well, see, it was the assistant warehouse foreman," Wally said. "Jimmy something-or-another. Or maybe it was Johnny. It could be Tommy. I'm not sure."

"We'll check it," I said.

Lawrence's cell phone rang and he answered the call. He listened for a few moments and then hung up.

"Lab said voice prints are too weak for comparison identification," Lawrence said.

"Did they compare the amplitude modulation against the frequency modulation for vibration patterns?" Wally said.

"I'm sure they did," Lawrence said. "Maybe."

"Even a professional voice scrambler can't disguise certain figurations of modulation," Wally said.

"Right. I know that," Lawrence said. "Excuse me for a minute."

Lawrence left the table to call his lab people.

"Very smart, Wally," I said.

"What?"

"What you just said."

"What did I say?"

"Leave room for dessert," I said.

# Chapter Eight

Robert picked us up in his company car at seven-thirty. He sat up front next to his driver. Lawrence and I occupied the back. We thought it best to leave Wally home as we didn't need him stressing out on us at the bank.

"The lab did that comparison thing Wally said and they have enough to match it up to the kidnapper if we catch him," Lawrence said.

*If.*

A powerful word, if.

If only I married him instead of you…

If only I took that job…

If only I bought that stock…

If, if, if—the world is a roadmap of if's. I know, I have a closet full of them.

The driver got us to the bank on 6th Avenue by 8:45 and dropped us off while he found a place to park.

I wished I had a cigarette. If only I hadn't quit.

The bank guard opened the door at nine and we entered along with several other customers. Lawrence showed the guard his FBI identification and asked to be taken to the branch president.

"I'm not sure I have that in bearer bonds on hand," he said. "I'll have the safe manager check."

"If you're short, can you have another bank deliver them?"

Lawrence said. "Maybe from Wall Street?"

"I suppose," the manager said. "I can also have the government—"

"That would take days," Lawrence said.

The manager sighed. "Let me go to the vault," he said.

Thirty minutes later, we watched as the manager counted fifteen minion dollars in bearer bonds in the vault room.

Robert exchanged the bonds for cash and we were on the way back to White Plains by eleven in the morning.

We reached the Sample office building by twelve-thirty.

"I'd like to put the bonds in your safe until later," Lawrence said.

"No problem," Robert said.

We found Wally in his office.

"I couldn't sit around the house all alone," Wally said. "I was going crazy."

"I understand," I said. "We got the bonds. What do you say we get some lunch?"

*   *   *

The Sample cafeteria served a decent lunch menu. We grabbed burgers with fries and large glasses of iced tea.

"Wally, I'd like to return to your condo after lunch," Lawrence said. "I want you to relax, maybe take a nap, watch TV, whatever. Point is, I want you calm and collected for tonight."

Wally nodded. "What are her chances?" he said.

"We pay the ransom, she has a good chance," Lawrence said.

Wally looked at me and I nodded.

*   *   *

While Wally took a nap, Lawrence and I took coffee to the condo balcony. It faced the backyard gardens, which were in full bloom.

"So far my people haven't been able to find anything on Barbara Bouchette in Pittsburgh," Lawrence said.

"We don't even know if that's her real name," I said.

"The tech guys are working on face recognition," Lawrence said. "If her mug shot is in the system, we'll find it."

"Did they check similar MOs in the system," I said.

"Of course. Maybe. I should mention that, huh?" Lawrence said.

"It can't hurt," I said.

"Why in God's name aren't you back on the job?" Lawrence said.

"The job doesn't want me," I said. "Besides, Jane is thinking of retiring."

'To do what? Take up knitting? Gardening," Lawrence said. "She's too young, and for that matter so are you to do nothing."

"The grey hairs on my head say different," I said. "Besides, I'm not doing nothing, I'm doing something right now."

"Maybe, but you could be doing a whole lot more," Lawrence said.

"Are your guys checking the master data bank for driver's license matches?" I said.

"Of course. Maybe. I'll see to it," Lawrence said.

"What time will your guys be here?" I said.

"I told them five."

"They're going to want dinner?" I said.

"We'll order takeout," Lawrence said.

*    *    *

After a pizza and garlic roll fest, there was nothing to do but wait for the call.

At one minute after eight, the phone rang. Equipment was turned on, our earpieces went in. Wally answered the call on the second ring.

"Hello," Wally said.

"Do you have the bonds?" the voice said.

"Yes," Wally said.

"Deliver them to the Shady Rest Motel off 95 in Yonkers, room 12 at midnight tonight," the voice said. "You'll be watched."

"Barbara?" Wally said.

"You'll receive instructions then," the voice said.

"I want to talk to—" Wally said as the voice hung up.

Lawrence turned to his men. "Find out where the Shady Rest Motel is," he said.

One of the men did a quick search on his laptop. "It's closed, sir. For renovations."

"That's just great," Lawrence said.

"Get a visual," I said.

The agent pulled up a satellite image of the Shady Rest Motel on his laptop. It was dark and deserted and in the process of renovation.

"I better change if I'm to deliver the bonds," Wally said.

"Are you crazy?" Lawrence said. "You're not leaving this apartment. We'll deliver the bonds."

"No, Paul, I will," I said.

"What? Jack, you're a civilian," Lawrence said.

"Where does it say a civilian can't deliver the ransom?" I said.

"When the FBI is on site, we—" Lawrence said.

"Give me a vest and I'll wear an earpiece," I said.

Lawrence sighed. "You heard the man, get him a vest," he said.

"And an earpiece," Wally said.

# Chapter Nine

I drove an FBI sedan onto 95 South from White Plains to Yonkers and followed the GPS unit to the Shady Rest Motel.

Lawrence and his crew were a hundred yards behind me in a black SUV.

I parked in the dark, deserted parking lot. Lawrence parked on the street. The motel was being gutted, but the doors to the rooms were still intact.

"Paul, can you hear me?" I said.

"Loud and clear, Jack. How's it looking?" Lawrence said in my earpiece.

"Like a deserted motel," I said. "I'm getting out with the briefcase and a flashlight."

I exited the sedan. "The door numbers have been removed and I'm counting doors," I said.

I walked to the twelfth door. "I'm entering room twelve," I said.

"Be careful, Jack," Lawrence said in my earpiece.

I pushed open the door and stepped inside and a motion detector triggered a light mounted to the wall.

"A motion detector triggered light came on," I said.

The room was empty except for an envelope taped to the wall.

"There is an envelope taped to the wall," I said.

"Be careful, Jack," Lawrence said in my earpiece.

I set the briefcase down on the floor and slipped on a pair of rubber gloves and removed the envelope taped to the wall. Inside was a typed letter.

"I have the note," I said. "I'm going to read it now."

"Go ahead," Lawrence said in my earpiece.

"Notice the camera on the wall to your left," I said. I looked at the small CCTV camera on the wall to my left. "Leave the bonds on the floor. If you want the stripper, go to the convenience store on Willard Avenue one block away and buy the last gallon of whole milk in the cooler."

"If that it?" Lawrence said in my earpiece.

"That's it," I said.

There were two gutted windows in the room. I backed out slowly to the door and returned to the car.

"I'm driving to you, Paul," I said.

*   *   *

I rode in the SUV with Lawrence and three of his men. The fourth man with him followed us in the sedan.

We found the all-night convenience store on Willard Avenue. Lawrence and I went in to buy the milk.

I opened the milk cooler and picked up the 6th carton of whole milk. There was a small envelope taped to the bottom. I removed the envelope, gave it to Lawrence and bought the milk.

We returned to the SUV where Lawrence opened the envelope. It contained a note and a key for a heavy-duty padlock.

The note read: *Storage locker number 88. The Lock and Key Storage on Bronxville Avenue.*

Lawrence programed the GPS unit and he drove us the four miles to the storage unit. It was just off the highway and practically in the woods. It was a self-service facility and we parked in front of unit 88. It was about the size of a one-car garage.

Lawrence used the key to open the massive padlock and we yanked the roll-up gate open enough for us to enter. There was a light switch and I flicked it on.

The only thing in the unit was a body bag on the floor.

Lawrence and I exchanged glances. We slipped on fresh latex gloves and unzipped the body bag.

It contained the nude, headless body of a woman. In addition, her hands had been severed.

"Jack, what I said about coming back on the job, forget I said it," Lawrence said.

Outside the unit, Lawrence barked orders to his men. "I want our people here within the hour and the body taken to our lab. Get the crime scene boys here right away and somebody find out who owns this place and get him out of bed."

"Paul, we need to return to the motel," I said. "Right now."

\* \* \*

We left Lawrence's men at the storage unit and took the sedan back to the motel.

The motion activated light had been removed, as well as the camera and briefcase,

"The windows," I said.

We left the room and went around back, using our flashlights to guide us. The rear of the motel was woods and beyond the woods was the highway.

"Somebody spent a great deal of time planning this," Lawrence said.

"Let's go, your guys can dust later," I said.

\* \* \*

After the body was transported to the FBI morgue in Manhattan, the lab men worked every square inch of unit 88.

Around four in the morning, the facility owner showed up. His name was Harold Walker. He was around sixty and grouchy from being woken up at three in the morning.

"What can I do for the FBI?" Walker said.

"You can tell us who rented unit 88," Lawrence said.

"That couldn't have waited until morning?" Walker said.

"No," Lawrence said.

"Come to the office," Walker said.

We followed Walker to the office located at the entrance to the units. Walker got behind his desk and checked his computer records.

"Unit 88 has been vacant for the past seven weeks," Walker said.

"Print out a list of everyone who has rented 88 for the past two years," I said.

We left the office with the list and returned to unit 88 where Lawrence's men were finishing up.

"Get over to the motel and dust the windows, walls and everything else and then check the perimeter for any Goddamn thing you can find," Lawrence said.

"Where are you going to be?" one of the man said.

"Sleeping until noon," Lawrence said. "Then you call me with anything you have."

Lawrence and I took the sedan and drove back to Wally's condo.

On the way, I said, "It's getting light out, Paul. Let's find a diner and get some breakfast."

The Front Street Diner was open twenty-four hours and we went in and grabbed a booth by the window. We ordered eggs, bacon, toast and coffee.

"What are we going to tell him, Jack?" Lawrence said.

"That we found a body," I said. "An unidentified body."

"Whoever organized this knew what they were doing," Lawrence said.

"There's something," I said. "There is always something."

"I'm afraid that's not going to be much comfort to Wally Sample," Lawrence said.

"No," I said. "It's not."

# Chapter Ten

Wally's reaction was expected. He had close to a full blown breakdown. I called Robert, who sent the company doctor over to the condo.

The doctor gave Wally a sedative to make him sleep for at least twelve hours and left the bottle with instructions.

Lawrence took the bedroom; I took the sofa bed and we both slept until noon.

I was up first and made coffee and sat out on the balcony. Lawrence, mug in hand, joined me a few minutes later.

"Wally is still asleep," I said.

Lawrence sipped coffee and nodded. "I have to call my people," he said.

"I'll make us some breakfast while you do that," I said.

Thirty minutes later, we sat down to omelets with bacon, hash browns, toast and orange juice.

"No prints on anything but traces of latex," Lawrence said. "Behind the motel they found shoe prints and a trail leading to the highway where a park and ride was located."

"Well planned out," I said.

"The previous renters of unit 88 all check out," Lawrence said. "No criminal records. All accounted for."

"The body?" I said.

"Still a Jane Doe," Lawrence said. "Without finger prints and a head, she will likely remain a Jane Doe."

"DNA," I said. "If your lab guys can find DNA in Bouchette's apartment and compare it to the Jane Doe for a positive."

"They are at her apartment right now," Lawrence said.

"Is anybody at the college?" I said.

"Two of my men," Lawrence said.

"How about we take a ride to the warehouse?" I said.

"What about Wally?" Lawrence said.

"Let me call his doctor," I said.

\* \* \*

The doctor came out of Wally's bedroom and found us in the living room.

"He's in a bad way, I'm afraid," the doctor said. "I put him to sleep again."

"For how long?" I said.

"At least another eight hours," the doctor said.

"Time enough to hit the warehouse," I said.

Lawrence drove the sedan to the Sample headquarters building where we met with Robert in his office.

"Naturally the entire family is upset with the events and of course for Wally," Robert said. "Our doctor called a bit ago and told me Wally is in bad shape."

"I'll stay with him again tonight," I said.

"Mr. Bekker, you have been a true friend to my brother," Robert said.

"Right now we need to see the warehouse manager," I said.

"That would be Ed Post," Robert said. "I assume it's about the bachelor party."

"We need some information," I said.

Robert wrote down the address for the warehouse. "Ed Post has been with us for a dozen years," he said. "He's a good man. I'll call and tell him you're coming."

"We'll fill you in later," I said.

\* \* \*

The Sample warehouse and distribution center was located in Yonkers on the border of Mount Vernon.

The one-store warehouse was about one hundred square feet in size and a massive operation, with six bays for trucks.

We had to sign in with a security guard at the front desk and then we were escorted to Ed Post's office. Along the way we passed massive brewing cauldrons, bottling conveyor belts and packing stations.

Ed Post was around fifty-years-old, a large man with a crew cut greying at the sides.

He stood from his desk and shook our hands.

"Bob told me on the phone," Post said. "I'm speechless."

"Maybe you could help us by answering a few questions," I said.

"Sure. Please grab a chair," Post said.

We took comfortable chairs opposite the desk as Post sat in his chair.

"How can I help?" he said.

"The bachelor party was when and for whom?" I said.

"Don Rivers, our floor supervisor in packing and shipping," Post said. "Everybody calls him Doc. The date was…"

Post paused to slip through his desk calendar. "Saturday, April 10."

"How many attended?" I said.

"Let's see," Post said. "Almost every male employee. That would be sixty-five."

"Who had the idea for the stripper cake?" I said.

"Some of Doc's friends, I think," Post said. "Everybody pitched in for food, drinks, gifts and the stripper."

"We want to talk to Rivers, but first could you tell us about the stripper," I said.

"Well, I wasn't in on that part at first," Post said. "Buy the boys convinced me so I went along. She was maybe twenty-five and a looker alright. After her dance, she got dressed and joined Mr. Sample at his table. They really hit it off. He was planning on marrying her. He must be devastated."

"Do you remember what company or club she worked for?" I said.

"No, but I'm sure the boys do," Post said.

"Okay, can you get Mr. Rivers now?" I said.

Post picked up his phone and asked for Rivers to report to his office.

Five minutes passed before Rivers knocked on the door.

"Come on in, Doc," Post said.

Rivers opened the door and entered the office. He was around thirty-five, with sandy hair, blue eyes and a slim build.

He looked at Lawrence and me and said, "Is there a problem, Ted?"

Lawrence stood and showed his identification to Rivers.

"FBI? Ted, what's going on?" Rivers said.

"The short of it is Miss Barbara Bouchette has been—" Lawrence said.

"Who?" Rivers said.

"The stripper from your bachelor party," Lawrence said.

"You mean Bubbles?" Rivers said. "Her?"

"That's who I mean," Lawrence said.

"What happened?" Rivers said.

"She was kidnapped three nights ago," Lawrence said. "The ransom was paid and in return was a decapitated body of a woman."

Rivers went a little green in the face for a moment. "Aw Jesus," he said. "Since he met her, Wally was like a new man. He comes around two, three times a week and I've never seen him happier. He told me he was going to marry her."

"Mr. Rivers, do you know the name of the company or club where she worked?" I said.

"I do not," Rivers said. "But I know the boys do."

"Ask them," I said.

"Sure."

Rivers left the office and was gone for ten or twelve minutes.

"How is Wally holding up?" Post said.

"Like you said earlier, devastated," I said.

"Despite his appearance and quirky way, he's something of a genus," Post said.

Rivers returned with a sheet of paper. "The boys tell me the Cupid's Retreat in Queens," he said and handed me the paper.

"Do you know who made the arrangements?" I said.

"Chuck Ludin, him and some of his friends," Rivers said.

"Let's go see Chuck," I said.

Rivers walked us to the packing line where Ludin worked.

"Chuck, these men need to see you for a minute," Rivers said.

Ludin looked at us. "My break isn't for…"

"Take ten," Rivers said.

"Is there somewhere we can talk privately?" Lawrence said.

"The break room," Rivers said.

Rivers led us to a large, cafeteria-type break room and left us at the door. The cafeteria was empty.

"We work two shifts," Ludin said. "Second shift goes to dinner at eight."

There was a self-service coffee machine and I got three cups of coffee and brought them to a vacant table.

"I assume since Doc asked me about the stripper, this is about her," Ludin said.

"Do you know she was planning to marry Wally Sample?" I said.

"Was?" Ludin said.

"She was kidnapped," I said.

"Oh God. Is she okay? Did you get her back?" Ludin said.

"No," I said. "What I want to ask you is how you came to hire her for the bachelor party."

"Oh, well, I went online and searched for strip clubs and called around and the Cupid's Retreat in Queens said they had girls available for party's provided it was agreed no one was to touch the girls," Ludin said,

"You called them?" Lawrence said.

"I did. I spoke to the manager and made the arrangements for one stripper," Ludin said. "They have these wooden cakes for the girl to pop out of if you pay for it."

"How much did it cost?" I said.

"Three hundred for the girl, another fifty for the cake," Ludin said.

"How did you pay?" I said.

"Credit card," Ludin said. "Everybody chipped in to pay the bill. I think I still have the statement for my credit card at home."

"Bring it to work," I said.

Ludin nodded.

"Did you know which girl would be coming?" Lawrence said.

"If you mean by name, I never did ask," Ludin said. "She was just supposed to be here by seven and she was."

"But she did give her stage name?" I said.

"Bubbles," Ludin said. "She said to call her Bubbles."

"Did anybody take video of the party, the cake and all that?" I said.

"Sure. Everybody."

"I want to see it," I said. "Bring it when you bring the receipt tomorrow."

"Sure thing."

"That's all for now," I said.

*　　*　　*

On the way back to Wally's condo, Lawrence got a call from his men with the news on DNA. They got clean DNA from the victim, but none from Barbara's apartment.

"How do you live in an apartment and not leave any DNA evidence?" Lawrence said. "On a toothbrush, hairbrush, something."

"I think we both know the answer to that, Paul," I said.

"Let's get back to Wally's," Lawrence said.

"Yeah."

# Chapter Eleven

When we returned to Wally's condo, we found Wally in his underwear in his bedroom trying to hang himself.

He had looped his belt, nailed one end to the top of the bathroom door and placed the loop around his neck.

"Don't try to stop me," Wally said.

Lawrence and I looked at him.

"Stand back," Wally said and sat down. On the floor. The belt was so long it barely tightened around Wally's neck.

"I could use some dinner," I said.

"Me too," Lawrence said.

"That's all you got to say, you want dinner?" Wally said.

"If you take the stupid belt off your neck, maybe you could join us?" I said.

Wally sighed and stood up and removed the belt. "Let me get dressed," he said.

\* \* \*

We ordered a hundred dollars' worth of Chinese food from a restaurant on Central Avenue and ate at the kitchen table.

"She's really gone, isn't she?" Wally said.

"Somebody is gone," I said. "We don't know who at this point."

"Why did they have to mutilate her like that?" Wally said.

"So we couldn't identify the body," I said.

"These people are sick," Wally said. "And they make me sick to my stomach so I can't even eat."

"You've eaten everything except the kitchen table," Lawrence said.

"I can't help it, I eat when I'm stressed," Wally said.

"Wally, was she a natural brunette?" I said.

"What do you mean natural?" Wally said.

"Women do dye their hair you know," I said. "Was her color natural?"

"I don't know," Wally said. "How would I know that?"

"What color was her pubic hair?" Lawrence said.

Wally paused for a second and then said, "I don't know, I never saw it."

"You mean you never had sex with the woman?" Lawrence said.

"She… we agreed to wait until the wedding," Wally said.

"I see," Lawrence said.

"It's not important right now," I said. "I want you to promise me you won't try anymore stunts like what you did with the belt."

"Obviously it didn't work," Wally said. "I'd cut my wrists but the sight of blood makes me sick."

"Wally, listen to me," I said. "We have a lot of work to do on this and we can't do it if we have to worry about you killing yourself."

"Mr. Bekker, we both know that I know what I am," Wally said. "My family is embarrassed by me, I have no friends and nobody cares if I'm here today and gone tomorrow, so don't worry about me. Nobody else does."

"Paul, tomorrow when we go out handcuff Wally to his bed," I said.

"In fact, I handcuff him tonight," Lawrence said.

"No, see, don't do that," Wally said. "I get rashes."

"A rash is better than being dead," I said.

"And I'm claustrophobic," Wally said.

"Your bedroom is bigger than my living room," I said.

"What if I have to go to the bathroom?" Wally said.

"A nice big old spaghetti pot should do the trick," I said.

"You don't give a guy any room, do you?" Wally said.

"Nope."

"Are you going to eat that last egg roll?" Wally said.

*    *    *

After dinner, while Wally took a shower, Lawrence and I took coffee to the balcony.

"I don't trust him," Lawrence said.

"Nope."

"We can't cuff him to the bed," Lawrence said.

"I know."

"We can't bring him with us," Lawrence said.

"Nope."

"We're going to be at this at least another three or four days, what do we do?" Lawrence said.

"I have an idea," I said.

I took out my cell phone and called home. Oz answered the hard line.

"When you coming home?" Oz said. "This dog and cat driving me crazy."

"Why?"

"The dog eat the cat food, the cat get mad and attack the dog, then the dog sleeps in the cat bed and the cat get mad and attack him again," Oz said.

"Where are they now?" I said.

"Both sleeping on Regan's bed."

"Where is Regan?"

"Working at the pet store."

"Listen, you're going to have a house guest," I said.

"Who?"

"Wally."

"Have you gone completely mad?" Oz said. "Last thing I need is that—"

"Let him stay in my room," I said.

"You mean you ain't coming with him?" Oz said.

"He tried to kill himself," I said. "Sort of."

"How you sort of try to kill yourself?" Oz said.

"He… never mind. Just keep an eye on him until I get back," I said. "Pick him up at the private airport."

"What time?" Oz said.

"I'll call you tomorrow," I said.

Oz sighed. "When Regan get home, we best go grocery shopping," he said.

"Clip coupons," I said.

"Clip coupons, my—" Oz said as I ended the call.

"Let's talk to Wally," I said.

We found him wearing pajamas in his bedroom.

"Please don't chain me to the bed," Wally said.

"I'm going to give you one of the doctor's sleeping pills," I said. "In the morning I want you to pack."

"Pack what?"

"A suitcase," I said. "You going to stay at my house."

"That old man doesn't like me," Wally said.

"He doesn't like anybody," I said. "Handcuffs or my house. Pick."

"Can I bring my laptop so I can work?" Wally said.

# Chapter Twelve

I was up with the sun, made coffee, drank a cup and then changed into sweats and running shoes.

I ran to the center of town and into a small park where I dropped and did one hundred push-ups on grass still wet with dew. Than I ran back to Wally condo. Round trip about four miles.

Lawrence was up and having coffee on the balcony. I joined him.

"Wally still asleep?" I said.

"Last time I checked."

I went for my cell phone and called Robert Sample, who had just arrived at the office. I told him my plan. He thought it was a good idea and would have the jet waiting at the airport.

"Let's go wake Wally," I said.

*　*　*

Wally looked at the Sample private jet.

"What if I promised not to hang myself again?" Wally said.

"Get on the plane, Wally," I said.

"I'm afraid of flying," Wally said.

"It's your plane. Get on it," I said.

"But—"

"I'll pick you up and carry you on," I said.

Wally sighed.

"Oz and my daughter will pick you up at the airport," I said.

"That old man hates me," Wally said. "He might try to kill me."

"Good, then it saves you the trouble," I said. "Get on the damn plane."

Wally sighed. "I don't like cats," he said. "Or dogs either. They make me sneeze."

"Wally, if you don't—" I said.

"I'm going," Wally said.

And he went.

"Jesus Christ," Lawrence said.

\*   \*   \*

It was too early to hit the strip club and Ludin's shift didn't start until three in the afternoon so we grabbed some lunch and then drove to The College of Westchester.

It was located on Central Avenue in the heart of White Plains. Enrollment in the private college was limited to about one thousand students and offered associate and bachelor's degrees.

I drove the sedan to the modern-looking campus and found a spot in guest parking.

We requested to see the Dean of Admissions.

Her name was Mary Moody and she was around fifty or so, with a nice face and smile. Lawrence showed her his identification and the smile quickly turned to a frown of concern.

"No need for you to be concerned," Lawrence said. "We're investigating a missing person who might have been enrolled here."

"Oh, I see," Mary said. "Well, what is her name?"

"Barbara Bouchette," Lawrence said.

Mary checked her computer. "Nobody by that name enrolled here," she said.

"Go back say ten years," Lawrence said.

Mary checked her computer records again. "A Laura Bouchette graduated in nineteen ninety-one."

"Take a look at her photograph," Lawrence said.

Lawrence showed Mary the photo we got from Wally.

"No, I can honestly say I've never seen this young lady in my life," she said.

"Thanks for your time," Lawrence said.

\* \* \*

I drove to the warehouse and we met Ed Post in his office.

"Has Chuck Ludin showed up for work yet?" I said.

"I'll get him," Post said.

After Post paged him, Ludin reported to his office.

"Here's the receipt and I have the video on my cell phone," Ludin said.

There was a small, flat screen television in the corner of the office.

"Can you show the video on the TV," I said.

"I don't think so, but on a laptop no problem," Ludin said.

"Use mine," Post said.

Ludin did what ever he did and then we gathered round the laptop to watch the video.

By the time the large cake was wheeled in on a dolly, most of the men at the bachelor party were half in the bag.

The lid of the cake popped open and out came Bubbles wearing a costume of balloons.

Her hair was pinned up and as she shimmed and swayed to her music, she removed a pin from her hair and one-by-one popped the balloons.

"Original," Lawrence said.

"There's Wally in the background," I said.

"He looks like he's in a trance," Lawrence said.

After all balloons had popped, Barbara wore just a G-string and pasties covering her nipples.

"She was supposed to leave now, but Wally asked her to stay," Ludin said. "There, see."

Wally walked up to Barbara and said something to her and she grabbed a robe from inside the cake, put it on and joined him at a table.

"That's it, that's all there is," Ludin said.

"Can you send that video to our phones" I said.

"Sure."

"Can you remember when she did leave?" I said.

"I was pretty wasted, but I think she stayed until the end and left with Wally," Ludin said.

"Okay, thank you," I said.

\* \* \*

"Want to grab dinner before or after we go to Queens?" I said.

"After," Lawrence said. "But I could use some coffee for the road."

We grabbed coffee at a diner near the warehouse and headed to Queens. The drive took over an hour. The Cupid's Retreat was located near Kennedy Airport on a back road.

It was a large, two-story building decorated in blue and red with white trim. All windows were darkened so you couldn't see in from the street.

A bouncer stood just inside the front door. The cover charge was fifteen dollars. Lawrence showed his identification to the bouncer.

"We need to see the manager for a few minutes," Lawrence said.

"I know nothing about nothing," the bouncer said.

"Who said you did? The manager," Lawrence said.

"I'll call him to the bar," the bouncer said.

We entered and went to the bar. It was about forty feet long with a runway where three dancers in G-strings and pasties strutted their stuff. The was also a center stage for the featured act.

A barmaid wearing a leopard print leotard approached us.

"We're waiting for the manager, but we'll take two ginger ales," I said.

She served two glasses of ginger ale and I left a twenty on the bar.

"I'm the manager," a man behind us said.

We turned and looked at him. He was a large, beefy man in his forties.

"Where can we talk privately?" Lawrence said.

"My office," the manager said.

We let the ginger ales on the bar and followed him down a hallway, past the bathroom and kitchen to his office.

The only chair in the office was behind his desk, so we stood.

"So what can I do for the FBI?" the manager said.

Lawrence showed him the photograph of Barbara Bouchette.

"Bubbles," he said. "Who's the little ferret with her?"

"I'll ask the questions," Lawrence said. "She work here?"

"She was a headliner," the manager said. "Did three fifteen minute shows a night, She really pulled them in with her balloon dance that one."

"Why did she quit?" Lawrence said.

"No idea," the manager said. "After about a year, she just stopped showing up."

"Did you try to call her?" Lawrence said.

"Sure, but her cell phone was disconnected."

"What name did she give you?" Lawrence said.

"Let me check her I-9," the manager said.

He rummaged through a file and produced the document and handed it to Lawrence.

"Make a copy of this for us," Lawrence said.

"Did she have a boyfriend?" I said.

"Who knows," the manager said. "She showed up, did her thing and went home."

"Any trouble from the customers?" I said.

"Why do you think I have six bouncers?" the manager said. "Most of them are moonlighting cops."

"Can we talk to some of the girls?" I said.

The manager stood up. "Follow me to the green room," he said.

The green room was the dressing room where six strippers were in various stages of undress.

"Ladies, the FBI," the manager said.

"Relax, ladies," Lawrence said. "We just have some questions about Barbara Bouchette."

"What about her?" a stripper said.

"Why did she quit?" Lawrence said.

"Who knows," another stripper said. "Girls come and go all the time."

"Did she ever talk about a boyfriend?" I said.

"Mister, in the business we're in, most of us want nothing to do with boyfriends," a stripper said.

"While you're getting ready to go on stage, you must talk to one another," I said.

"Not that one," a stripper said. "She kept to herself."

"You girls all use the same dressing room, right. Was Barbara a natural brunette?" I said.

"You mean did her drapes match her rug?" a stripper said.

"That's what I mean," I said.

"She was a natural redhead," a stripper said. "But she changed her hair color every few months it seemed."

"Did she ever mention attending college?" I said.

"Not to us," a stripper said.

"Alright, thank you ladies," Lawrence said.

We followed the manager back to his office.

"Do the girls draw a salary?" I said.

"The keep seventy percent of their tips," the manager said. "It's up to them to pay their own taxes."

"How much can they make?" I said.

"Three to four hundred an eight hour shift on a regular night," the manager said. "Six hundred on Saturday."

"How many shifts do they work?" I said.

"Most girls want only three," the manager said. "They're feet hurt after eight hours, so they say."

"And Bubbles?" I said.

"She was a headliner," the manager said. "Private room only. Tickets are fifteen dollars and one drink minimum. Maximum is one hundred and twenty five. She sold out every show. She got a third of the ticket price and her tips were her own."

Lawrence took out the receipt from Ludin and showed it to the manager. "How often do the girls rent out for a private show?" he said.

"Three or four bachelor parties a month," the manager said. "Same split on the flat fee, they keep their tips."

"Do you remember this one?" Lawrence said.

"Honestly, I don't remember any of them."

"How do you decide which girl to send?" I said.

"I ask them," the manager said. "Someone always volunteers."

"So it's a voluntary…" Lawrence said.

"Wait. Hold on," the manager said. "Now that I think about it this was the first time Bubbles volunteered. And she gave up her second and third private show to do it. She said it would be a nice change. Soon after that, she quit. Too bad, she was a top earner."

"Make a copy of her I-9 and we'll be on our way," Lawrence said.

# Chapter Thirteen

I bit into a thick, bacon burger and said, "What are the odds the information on the I-9 is false."

"I wouldn't take that bet," Lawrence said.

"When you check the information on the I-9, also check with the IRS if she filed taxes," I said.

"First thing in the morning," Lawrence said.

After dinner and before a slice of apple pie, I called home.

"Hey, Dad," Regan said.

"How did it go at the airport?" O said.

"Wally kissed the tarmac."

"Kissed the… literally?" I said.

"Got down on his knees and kissed the ground," Regan said.

"How is he now?" I said.

"Well, he treated us to takeout dinner," Regan said. "Fried chicken with mashed potatoes, Chinese food and pizza."

"Good Lord," I said.

"Right now he's passed out on the sofa with Cuddles sleeping on his stomach and Molly sleeping in his hair," Regan said.

"Is Oz around?" I said.

"In his easy chair. We're watching Ray Donovan," Regan said.

"I don't want you watching…" I said and Oz came on the line.

"The little butterball sleeping," Oz said.

"I don't want her watching Ray Donovan," I said.

"Who watchin' that?" Oz said. "We watchin' *End Game* with a bunch of super heroes in tights jumping around like circus performers."

"But she said… never mind," I said. "Just do me a favor and keep a close eye on Wally until I get back."

"The Teletubby sleeping on the sofa. He got a hole in his sock," Oz said.

"Never mind the—" I said.

"Boy wearing one black sock and one red one?" Oz said.

"I should be home in two days," I said. "Just keep an eye on him."

I hung up and ate my apple pie.

"How's Wally?" Lawrence said.

"He has a hole in his sock," I said.

*　*　*

Lawrence went to bed early, I took a glass of milk to the balcony and sat to think for a while.

The backyard garden was in full bloom and I could smell the various flowers. A floodlight illuminated below and I could see benches and a Lilly pond.

The chances of the information on the I-9 document being real were a million to one shot. Was Barbara volunteering for the bachelor party, the only time she did so, a coincidence?

Was the entire kidnapping scheme thought out by some master criminal and if so, who's body was in unit 88 if not Barbara Bouchette?

If not her body we found, she had to be in on the entire plan.

Where does one happen to get a headless, handless dead women to use as a stand in?

Why dye your hair brunette?

Wally would have no way of knowing what color your hair is and neither would patrons at the strip club?

Why Pittsburgh?

You could pick any city in the country, why Pittsburgh?

Targeting Wally wasn't an accident. He might be a squirrely little genius, but he was also worth upwards of a billion dollars.

Did she tell Wally she went to college to make herself more appealing to Wally? He wouldn't care one way or the other.

I finished my milk and went to sleep on the sofa bed.

\* \* \*

I woke up around two in the morning, got up for a minute to write myself a note.

*Check the Bouchette apartment one more time.*

Then I went back to sleep.

# Chapter Fourteen

I was up before Lawrence, made coffee, took a cup on the balcony and then went for a run afterward.

I ran to the park, did one hundred push-ups on the grass and then found a sturdy tree branch and used it to do pull-ups. I did three sets of fifteen reps each set and then did some extra push-ups before running back to Wally's apartment.

Lawrence was on the balcony with a mug of coffee. I joined him.

"Call your guys?" I said.

"They should have reports from the IRS and on the I-9 by noon," Lawrence said.

"Autopsy report on the body?" I said.

"This afternoon sometime."

"After breakfast, I want to see the Bouchette apartment again," I said.

\* \* \*

The moment we entered the Bouchette apartment, I had the same feeling I had from the first visit.

Something was out of place. Missing. I couldn't put my finger on it and I knew it would bother me until I figured it out.

"What are you looking for?" Lawrence said.

"I don't know, Paul," I said.

"Let me know when you find it," Lawrence said.

I started in the kitchen. There were four cupboards above the counter. Dishes were neatly stacked, as were glasses and cups. Cupboards below the counter held neatly stacked appliances. The silverware drawer held perfectly aligned knives, forks and spoons.

The refrigerator held a six-pack of soda, six-pack of beer and a gallon of ice cream, all unopened.

There wasn't one thing out of place in the entire kitchen.

I moved on to the bathroom. It was, like the kitchen, as neat as a pin. No mess on the sink. None of the typical junk women usually keep. Jane has so much stuff on her sink it's dangerous to brush your teeth. The linen closet contained neatly folded sheets, pillow cases and towels.

An unused bar of soap was in the shower. A bottle of shampoo and conditioner rested on a shelf in the shower, both unopened.

The medicine chest held hardly anything useful. Not even a bottle of aspirin.

Lawrence followed me to the bedroom. The closet held clothing hung neatly on hangers. Perfectly aligned shoes lined the closet floor.

The bed was perfectly made.

"Sterile," I said.

"What?" Lawrence said.

"This apartment might as well be a dollhouse," I said. "The entire place is nothing but a prop to fool Wally. She probably never even slept here."

"It's looking that way," Lawrence said.

"There isn't a note, a scrap of paper, nothing to say a woman lived here," I said.

"Seen enough?" Lawrence said.

"For now."

"I'd like to make Manhattan before lunch," Lawrence said.

* * *

Lawrence drove the sedan to the FBI Regional Office in Manhattan.

An agent made a report on the I-9. "The Social Security number and address are false," he said. "According to the Social Security Department, that particular number has never been used. The address seems to be totally made up."

"Never been used doesn't mean it doesn't exist," I said. "What's its origin?"

The agent looked at his report. "Pennsylvania," he said. "But like I said, it's never been used."

"And the IRS report?" I said.

"Taxes have never been paid on that account," the agent said.

"Let's go see the ME," I said.

* * *

"I identified what removed her head and hands," the ME said. "A chain saw."

"Well that's lovely," Lawrence said.

"She's between twenty-five and twenty-eight-years-old," the ME said. "Estimated height is five-foot-six, weight is one forty."

"Pubic hair?" I said.

"Redhead," the ME said.

I looked at Lawrence and he nodded.

"Cause of death, despite what you might thing, was not having her head cut off," the ME said. "That bit of fun came later. This poor creature was born with a defective heart that apparently went undetected. She died of a heart attack."

The next obvious question was, "Where?"

"You're the detective," the ME said.

\* \* \*

We stopped for lunch at a diner a few blocks from the FBI building in Manhattan. The diner specialized in burgers served on English muffins.

"I don't know who that poor woman is but it certainly isn't Barbara Bouchette," I said.

"Jack, even Barbara Bouchette isn't Barbara Bouchette," Lawrence said.

"So what now?" I said.

"We'll talk to Robert Sample and then the regional office in New York takes over," Lawrence said.

"Which is another way of saying whoever did this has gotten away with it," I said.

"Have faith, Jack," Lawrence said.

"How many unsolved kidnapping cases are on the books, Paul?" I said. "How many FBI Agents are tied up with foreign and domestic terrorist cases? Bank fraud? Extortion? Organized crime cases? What's one more unsolved kidnapping case?"

"Well, when you put it that way," Lawrence said.

"Yeah."

\* \* \*

Robert, Steven, Susan, Amy and Barbara met us in the conference room at the Sample iced Tea building.

"As I knew it, we threw fifteen million dollars away on Wally's little whore's blackmail scheme," Barbara said.

"The investigation is far from over," Lawrence said.

"How's the Hoffa investigation going?" Barbara said. "Find him yet?"

"Barbara, that's not fair," Robert said.

"Let me assure you the FBI will do everything in it's power to find and bring to justice those responsible," Lawrence said.

"Responsible for what?" Barbara said.

"Mr. Bekker, how long will you keep Wally with you?" Robert said.

"Forever comes to mind," Barbara said.

"Until I'm sure he's no longer suicidal," I said.

"Thank you for that," Robert said.

\* \* \*

After packing my suitcase, Lawrence and I locked up Wally's condo.

"Give you a ride home?" Lawrence said. "I just happen to have a jetliner standing by at the airfield."

"Beats walking," I said.

# Chapter Fifteen

My car was in the private airfield's long term parking garage. Lawrence had a few minutes to kill before his jetliner could take off again, so he walked with me to my car.

"Don't go nuts now, Jack," Lawrence said. "I know how you get when something gets under your skin. Let the regional office handle things. Okay?"

"Sire," I said.

"I mean it, Jack," Lawrence said.

"I know," I said.

"What's the use of talking to you," Lawrence said.

"I didn't say anything," I said.

"It's the nothing you didn't say that says it all," Lawrence said.

"What does that even mean?" I said.

We reached my car and I fished out my keys.

"How old is that rust bucket?" Lawrence said.

"Fifteen years and there's hardly any rust," I said.

We shook hands.

"Call we when you do what you say you're not going to do," Lawrence said.

"I won't," I said.

I got behind the wheel of my rust bucket and drove home.

*   *   *

If I was expecting a big welcome home, I didn't get it. The only one home was Molly the cat and she barely looked up from her nap on the sofa.

It was dinner time so my guess was that they went out to a restaurant and took Cuddles with them.

I changed into sweats and went to the backyard. My body was stiff and achy from sitting, driving and flying.

I sectioned off an area in the backyard for a weight bench and dumbbell rack, a heavy bag and speed bag, a pull-up station, elevated push-up bars and a space to jump rope. I built an awning over everything for rainy days.

Jumping rope for ten minutes limbered me up. Then came a half dozen sets of bench presses with dumbbells. I switched out with fifteen minutes on the heavy bag, another fifteen on the speed bag, six sets of pull-ups and six sets of elevated push-ups.

The sky was darkening when Regan's car pulled into the driveway behind mine. I toweled off and went to the living room.

"Hey, Dad," Regan said.

Cuddles ran past me, jumped on the sofa and snuggled with Molly.

"Mr. Bekker, you're back," Wally said.

"Thank God," Oz said.

"We went out to dinner," Regan said. "If we knew you were coming back we would have brought you something."

"It's alright, honey," I said. "I'm going to grab a shower and then I want to talk to Wally for a bit."

After a shower, I tossed on a clean warm-up suit and returned to the kitchen. Regan had made a pot of coffee. I filled a mug and entered the living room where Regan and Wally were playing a video game. Oz was in his recliner.

"Wally, let's talk," I said.

"Oz, take his place," Regan said.

Oz took over for Wally while we went to the backyard and took chairs at the patio table.

"Wally, I want you to know the FBI is continuing the investigation," I said.

Wally nodded.

"The other thing is that there is no doubt that the dead woman from unit 88 is definitely not Bubbles," I said.

"So Barbara's alive," Wally said gleefully. "I knew she couldn't be—"

"Hold on, Wally," I said. "We don't know what happened or where she is at this point. The main thing is—"

"Find her, Mr. Bekker. Please find her," Wally said.

"Wally, listen to me," I said. "She—"

"You're a detective. I want to hire you to find her," Wally said. "I don't care what it costs, just find her."

"Wally, you don't understand," I said. "It's not that simple."

"If you won't do it I'll do it myself," Wally said. "Or I'll hire another detective. How hard could that be?"

"Give me a day to mull it over," I said. "Right now I need some food."

"Thank you, Mr. Bekker," Wally said.

Wally returned to the video game. I grabbed some frozen burgers from the freezer and fired up the grill.

While I was grilling, I called Jane on my cell phone.

"Are you home?" she said.

"Got in a little while ago," I said. "Free for dinner tomorrow night?"

"My place or eat out?"

"Either is fine."

"My place," Jane said. "So how did it go with Wally's kidnapping?"

"Long story. I'll fill you in tomorrow," I said.

"Seven o'clock and don't be late," Jane said.

After we hung up, I called Walt.

"You back?" Walt said.

"I'm back," I said.

"And?"

"Long story."

"That's not good," Walt said.

"What?"

"Whenever you say long story it usually means you want my help," Walt said.

"Not this time," I said. "Paul has the New York regional office assigned to the case," I said.

"Uh huh," Walt said.

"When did you become so skeptical?" I said.

"When we first became partners twenty-five-years ago," Walt said.

"I'll see you tomorrow," I said.

"Don't come empty handed," Walt said.

My burgers were done. I went to the kitchen and returned with a can of ginger ale and ate at the patio table.

Barbara Bouchette, who and where are you?

Who is the dead woman?

Who has the fifteen million in bearer bonds?

Who set the whole thing in motion?

It was out of my hands.

And in the hands of the FBI.

There was nothing more I could do except sit back and hope for the best.

The kitchen sliding door opened and Regan came out with a mug of coffee and set it on the patio table.

"I just made it," she said.

"Thanks, honey," I said.

"Dad, Wally is a complete mess," Regan said. "Half the time he doesn't know what day it is. He wears two different colored socks and would forget to comb his hair if you didn't tell him to. He can't work a toaster, but he can do the most complex math problems in his head in the blink of an eye."

"I know all that," I said.

"He needs your help, Dad," Regan said.

"I know," I said.

Regan patted my shoulder. "Good," she said. "Oh, by the way, I made up the day bed for you in the basement."

# Chapter Sixteen

Regan made breakfast. Waffles with bacon, orange juice and coffee.

"I have to work four hours at the pet store today," Regan said.

I looked at Oz.

"I ain't no baby sitter," Oz said.

"Don't worry about me," Wally said. "I can take care of myself."

"Wally, you wearing a dress shirt with panama pants and one sock," Oz said.

Wally paused with a mouthful of waffles and looked at his feet. "I know," he said.

"We find something to do to keep you occupied," Oz said.

After breakfast, I went for a workout in the backyard. An hour later, I hopped the fence and went for a run along back roads that led to the beach open to the public. It wasn't a beach morning, with the temperature around fifty-five degrees.

Working out and thinking are synonymous to me. Many a case was solved in my mind during a long run or when pounding the heavy bag.

Once it's solved in your mind, you have direction and focus.

This mess that Wally dumped in my lap had neither.

My faith in Paul Lawrence is unyielding. The FBI not so much. The amount of work dumped on their collective laps was the size of Mount Everest. By the time they freed up the manpower to get to Wally's case, I would be drawing Social Security.

Having worked a thousand investigations, experience taught that when faced with an unsolvable case the thing to do was to go back to the beginning and start anew.

When I returned home, Regan had left for the pet store. Oz was in his recliner, reading a book. Wally, one barefoot and all was seated on the sofa with his laptop on the coffee table.

Molly was sleeping on Wally's lap. Cuddles was curled up beside him.

I took a shower and changed and returned to the living room.

"I'll be out for a while," I said.

Oz looked at me.

"Don't worry," he said.

\* \* \*

"Let me see if I got this straight," Walt said as he chomped on a bacon cheeseburger. "Bubbles, Wally's would be bride, doesn't exist anywhere on paper. You got a headless, handless woman who isn't Bubbles in a storage unit. Bubbles pays no taxes, has a fake social Security number and somewhere out there is fifteen million in bearer bonds floating around. Is that about it?"

"Pretty much," I said.

"And you haven't solved it yet?" Walt said.

"By the time the FBI whittles down their caseload and actually takes a shot at it, Wally will be eligible for retirement," I said.

"It sounds like the FBI got beat," Walt said.

"Wally wants to hire me," I said.

"Of course he does," Walt said.

"I don't have the resources the FBI does," I said.

"Neither do I," Walt said. "And certainly Jane doesn't."

"So," I said.

"Yeah, so," Walt said.

"Are you going to help me or not?" I said.

"With what?" Walt said. "You got beat. It happens. Eighty percent of all murders go unsolved, you know that."

"But are you going to help me or not?"

"Of course I'm going to help you," Walt said. "Now pay the check."

\* \* \*

"Wally?" I said.

He looked up from his laptop. "Did you know the driving distance for one of our trucks is four hundred and eighty four miles and the average truck will spend close to two hundred dollars on gas each way," he said. "If you factor in the salary of the driver, wear and tear on the truck and putting him up for the night, it might be cheaper to ship product by train."

"That's interesting, Wally," I said. "Right now I..."

"I have to send a memo to Robert," Wally said.

"Can that wait for a minute? I want to talk to you," I said.

Wally sat back on the sofa.

"I'm going to do whatever I can to find the kidnapper," I said.

Wally looked at me.

"I'd like you to fill out the necessary forms to hire me so that you are legally my client," I said.

"Forms?" Wally said.

"It's necessary for you to hire me," I said. "Client, detective privilege and all that."

"Okay," Wally said.

I had the forms ready and set them on the coffee table. Wally read them and said, "How much do I pay you?" he said.

"One dollar," I said.

"One dollar?"

"Wally, I'm not going to charge you for this," I said. "You are a friend of the family. I'll keep track of expenses and you can pay those. Now please fill out the forms."

"I need a…"

I handed Wally a pen. He signed both forms and handed them back to me.

"Wait, I don't have a dollar," Wally said.

"Pay me when you have it," I said. "Where is Oz?"

"In the backyard with the dog."

"Okay, go send your memo."

"What memo?" Wally said.

"The one… never mind."

I entered the backyard through the kitchen door. Oz was tossing a tennis ball to Cuddles.

"Oz," I said as I went to the patio table.

"Take five, mutt," Oz said.

He came to the table and we took chairs. Cuddles stayed beside Oz and sat with the tennis ball in his mouth.

"I have to go out for a while," I said. "Keep an eye on Wally for me."

"When you gonna keep an eye on him?" Oz said. "He your boy."

"I know, but I have to work this thing," I said. "I promised him."

"I gained five pounds since he be here," Oz said. "And we haven't had to cook dinner in a week. I'll be three hundred pounds before he leave."

"I have to grab a shower before I go out," I said.

"Tell Jane I said hi," Oz said.

# Chapter Seventeen

I was about ready to fall asleep when Jane shook me. "Oh no you don't," she said. "I have all that food I made that needs to be eaten."

I sat up in her bed.

She grabbed my shirt and put on a pair of white socks.

I tossed on my T-shirt and shorts.

We went to the kitchen.

"We have chicken parm, garlic rolls and ginger ale," Jane said. "And gelato for dessert. Give me a minute to heat things up."

As she nuked the food, Jane lit a cigarette. After a couple of puffs, she handed it to me. "Don't worry, I won't tell Regan," she said.

I started smoking when I started drinking. I kicked the drinking, but the smoking lingered on like a rash that never quite goes away.

Jane served dinner and I told her about Bubbles.

"Wow. That's quite a mess," Jane said. "What do you plan on doing about it?"

"I don't know. Something," I said.

"Something could mean shopping for underwear," Jane said.

"Thing is, I'm not really sure I can do much more than what's already been done," I said. "And I certainly don't have the resources the FBI does."

"Are you sure about that?" Jane said. "I've seen you solve some cases I thought unsolvable. And without the resources of the FBI or even my little department."

"The only thing I'm sure about is we have a woman without a head, a stripper that doesn't exist and somebody has fifteen million in bearer bonds," I said.

"Have you backed Walt into a corner yet?" Jane said.

"Kicking and screaming, but yes," I said.

"Well, I don't know what a county sheriff can do to help, but just ask," Jane said.

"There is one thing," I said.

"Does it have to do with your case?"

"Not a thing," I said.

Jane gave me her sensual look. "Does it involve returning your shirt?"

"You can leave it on if you want to, but—"

Jane grabbed my hand. "Time's a wasting," she said and yanked me to the bedroom.

\* \* \*

After a shower, I got dressed and Jane and I had a cup of coffee at her kitchen table.

"Regan will be twenty if a few months, Jack. I don't think it would be too much of a shock to her if you stayed over," Jane said.

"Twenty going on fourteen," I said. "Besides, I don't want her to think less of you as her would be stepmother."

"And when is that event happening?" Jane said.

"As soon as you pull the pin and retire," I said.

"That sounds like blackmail," Jane said.

I sipped some coffee and thought for a moment.

"What?" Jane said.

"What size are your... you know?" I said and pointed.

"The milk bottles?"

"That's one way of putting it."

"Thirty-eight D and I'm not an ounce over one forty-five," Jane said. "Sometimes. Why?"

"Have a look at Bubbles," I said.

I showed Jane the video of Bubbles from the bachelor party.

"What size is she?" I said.

"Double D, but they're fake," Jane said.

"Fake? Are you sure?" I said.

"Jack, they don't even so much as move," Jane said. "I could balance a coffee mug on them. They're fake."

I scrolled through my work photos and showed Jane the woman from unit 88.

"I've seen her look better," Jane said.

"What size is she?" I said.

"Maybe thirty-four B," Jane said.

I put my phone away. "I better get going," I said.

"Thanks for the nightmares," Jane said.

\* \* \*

The daybed in the basement wasn't the worst bed I've ever slept in, but it was far from the best. Still, tired enough, it did the trick.

What kept me awake wasn't the bed. It was Bubbles' fake breasts. The kidnapper had to know a comparison of the two women would they weren't the same woman. It was a mistake on his part.

The first one he's made so far.

I fell asleep thinking about that.

# Chapter Eighteen

In the morning, I made breakfast. Scrambled eggs with bacon and potatoes, toast and orange juice.

"Wally, you're looking pale," I said.

"I am?" Wally said.

"Uh oh," Regan said.

"What's uh oh?" Wally said.

"Never mind," I said. "I'm taking you to the beach for some fresh air and sunshine."

"I hate the beach," Wally said.

"As soon as it warms up, we're going," I said. "All of us."

"That mean me, too?" Oz said. "I ain't pale. I ain't never been pale my whole life."

"A little fresh air and sun won't do you any harm," I said.

After breakfast, I did a workout in the backyard. The physical activity freed up my thoughts and allowed me to focus.

Around noon, I shook Oz awake on his easy chair. "Let's go," I said.

"We the pale beach-bound Brady Bunch," Oz said. "'Cept me."

\* \* \*

I parked in the municipal lot and we walked to the beach. I carried four folding chairs, Regan the picnic basket, Wally his laptop. Cuddles followed on his leash, held by Oz.

Twice Wally tripped on the sand.

"What's the matter with you boy, you tripping on nothing," Oz said.

"Dad, they're gone," Regan said. "The trailers are gone."

"I know honey," I said. "But we'll buy a condo as soon as the initial listing is posted."

We stopped where our trailer used to be and set up the chairs.

"Who wants to go for a run?" I said.

"Only nobody ever," Oz said. "So go on and bake yourself."

I took off along the water. The sun was warm, the breeze light and I ran for about two and a half miles before I stopped and pulled my cell phone from the back pocket of my shorts.

I called Paul Lawrence.

"I was wondering when the first call would come," Lawrence said.

"Paul, go back and look at the bachelor party again," I said. "Bubbles, her breasts are fake."

"How do you know?" Lawrence said.

"Show them to any female agent if you don't believe me," I said.

"Okay, they're fake. So what?"

"The woman in unit 88, her breasts are real," I said. "So our kidnapper has made one mistake. Where there is one there are others."

"What are you thinking, Jack?" Lawrence said.

"I'll let you know when I think it," I said.

I hung up and turned around.

Why that woman? Why not a woman with larger fake breasts to make it appear the real Bubbles was the victim in unit 88?

Why…?

I paused and called Lawrence back.

"Did they run down the names of the previous renters of unit 88?" I said.

"They did and it's a no go on any of them."

"Thanks."

I hung up and continued running.

When I returned to the group, Regan and Wally were playing Frisbee with Cuddles and Oz was sitting in a folding chair.

I sat beside him.

"They always make a mistake," I said. "Sooner or later."

"If you mean only everybody, I agree," Oz said.

"That's all it takes is one," I said.

"You talking about potato chips or people?" Oz said.

"If they make one, they've made two," I said.

"What in blazes you talking about?" Oz said.

"Fake breasts," I said.

"At my age I'd rather the potato chips," Oz said.

"Why not find a victim with fake breasts to make it appear as if it was the real Bubbles?" I said.

"A question for the ages," Oz said.

I looked at the ocean. "Any port in a storm," I said.

Regan and Wally walked to us. "Lunchtime, Dad," Regan said.

We had chicken and turkey sandwiches, a giant bag of chips, pickles, the extra crunchy kind and cans of ginger ale.

Cuddles had a bowl of water and some dog treats.

After lunch, Regan, Cuddles and Wally resumed their game of Frisbee.

"Oz," I said. "What port do you go to for a dead body?"

"Man, I still working on the fake breasts thing," Oz said.

# Chapter Nineteen

Besides the daybed in the basement, I had an office, a sofa with a television and some extra gym equipment.

I sat at my desk with a mug of coffee and wished I had a cigarette. If only I hadn't quit.

If only.

There it was again. If only.

Any port in a storm.

Say you needed a dead body for a kidnapping scheme, where would you go to get one. It's not as if dead body's were just hanging around on street corners.

I picked up the landline phone and called Paul Lawrence.

"Three times a charm," Lawrence said after a ten minute wait.

"Your Muzak is terrible," I said.

"You don't like Kenny G?" Lawrence said.

"Where do you go to get a dead body?" I said.

"Ah, a Jeopardy question," Lawrence said.

"Places are limited, where do you go?" I said.

The was a long pause and I heard the gears turning in his mind. "The morgue and hospitals," he said.

"I doubt our kidnapper would risk a long drive with a corpse in his car," I said. "Do a search of hospitals and morgues in New York State, New jersey and Connecticut."

'That's a lot of ground to cover," Lawrence said.

"You got a lot of agents," I said. "Target women between twenty and thirty with heart conditions."

"Call you back late tomorrow," Lawrence said.

"I'll be here late tomorrow," I said.

Regan entered the basement through the connecting door off the kitchen and came halfway down the stairs.

"Dad, dinner," she said.

"Be right there," I said.

Dinner was chicken fried steak with gravy, mashed potatoes, corn and biscuits.

"Who eat like this?" Oz said. "Wally, are you aware of the cholesterol ongoing problem in this country?"

"It's yummy," Wally said.

"Course it yummy," Oz said. "Cause it bad for you."

"We got ice cream for dessert," Regan said.

"Of course you do," Oz said.

After dinner, Oz and I took dishes of chocolate ice cream and mugs of coffee to the backyard.

"How is he?" I said.

"If you mean health wise, I give him about a month," Oz said. "If you mean is he suicidal, he ain't at the moment."

"But that could change?"

"Sure, so can the weather," Oz said. "Right now he preoccupied with some logistics problem. When he solve that he might focus on the girl again."

"You're saying I should keep him here a while longer?" I said.

"God help me but yeah," Oz said.

"Okay."

"It ain't okay but what else you gonna do," Oz said.

Regan entered the backyard. "Oz, Wally is working on some problem, feel like a game?" she said.

"Be there in a minute," Oz said.

"I'll set it up," Regan said and went inside.

"One thing you don't want on your conscience is that boy suicide," Oz said.

He went inside and I sat for a few minutes thinking. Say you wanted to remove a body from the morgue, how would you go about it sight unseen?

Same for a hospital.

There is always somebody around, watching. A security guard, morgue attendant, police, doctors and nurses, EMTs, not to mention surveillance cameras.

With all those eyes, how do you sneak a body out of a hospital or morgue?

My cell phone rang and I removed it from my pocket.

"I'm taking tomorrow off," Jane said. "Want some company?"

"What did you have in mind?" I said.

"Something fun. Maybe a picnic in the park with Regan and Oz?"

"And Wally."

"Yeah, that too."

"Noon?"

"I'll be there. We'll take my SUV."

After hanging up with Jane, I went inside and found Regan and Oz playing a video game in the living room.

"Jane wants to have a family picnic in the part tomorrow," I said.

"Cool," Regan said.

"Where's Wally?" I said.

"In your room," Regan said.

I went to my bedroom. Wally was at my desk, working on something on his laptop.

"Family outing tomorrow," I said. "With Jane."

"The woman sheriff?" Wally said.

"So do me a favor and try to wear socks that match," I said.

I went to the basement, stripped down and got into the daybed.

I spent half the night trying to figure out how to sneak a corpse out of a hospital or morgue.

# Chapter Twenty

"If you wanted to sneak a corpse out of a hospital or a morgue, how would you go about it?" I said.

"You really are a fun date," Jane said.

We were in a park not far from my house. While Regan and Wally tossed a Frisbee around with Cuddles, Oz took a nap on the blanket next to ours.

The picnic basket was filled with fried chicken, potato chips, slaw, salad, ginger ale and chocolate cake.

I friend the chicken. Regan made the slaw and chocolate cake.

"So, how would you do it?" I said.

"I wouldn't," Jane said. "Now without getting caught."

"Unless?" I said.

"Unless," Jane said and looked at me. "I worked there."

"Yeah," I said.

"Want to sneak away for a smoke?" Jane said.

"Regan has a nose like a bloodhound," I said.

"Who's the adult here?" Jane said.

Without opening his eyes, Oz said, "It ain't him."

"Cover for us," I said.

"Man, they ain't paying you the slightest mind," Oz said.

We snuck away to the cover of a large tree about fifty feet away. Jane lit up and took several puffs before handing me the cigarette.

"You're a bad influence on me," I said.

"Imagine if you had me full time the damage I could do," Jane said.

We heard Regan scream. I dropped the cigarette and we turned and ran back. Oz was attempting to retrieve the Frisbee from two overzealous young me. One of the men had Wally in a head lock.

"You leave him alone," Regan said.

"Or what?" the man holding Wally said.

"My dad will kick the crap out of you, that's what," Regan said.

"Who's your dad?" the man said.

"Me," I said and came up behind Regan.

The man holding Wally stepped back and stuck his right hand in his pocket.

"Go ahead and pull that knife," I said. "And I'll make you eat it."

"We meant no harm," the other man said. "We was just funning."

"Go funning somewhere else," I said.

They turned and walked away along a path.

"Thanks, Dad," Regan said. She sniffed me and said, "Jane!"

"What?" Jane said. "I'm minding my own business here."

"Let's eat," I said.

"Best idea all day," Oz said.

We ate on the blankets and talked about Regan's job at the pet store, Jane's thoughts of retirement, Wally's latest theory on winning the lottery and why Oz's feet hurt when he's trying to sleep at night.

Somehow, the chocolate cake was intact and we ate slices on paper plates with plastic forks.

After lunch, we played an all hands on deck game of Frisbee with Cuddles.

It was after five by the time I drove us back to my house.

"Jane, stay for dinner," Regan said.

"Only if I can help," Jane said.

While I grabbed a workout in the backyard, Oz grabbed a nap, Cuddles and Molly wrestled on the lawn, Wally tackled work on his laptop and Jane and Regan had a talk in the kitchen.

Near the end of my workout when I was doing speed bag work, Paul Lawrence called on my cell phone.

I grabbed it from the patio table.

"Saint Joseph's Hospital in the Bronx," Lawrence said. "I'm leaving tomorrow, feel like meeting me there?"

"I'll grab a flight in the morning," I said.

"Still have a fax machine?"

"Who doesn't?"

"I'll fax over a preliminary report in a few minutes," Lawrence said.

I finished my speed bag work and went to my basement office. The fax was just coming through the machine on my desk.

The basement has a sink, counter, small refrigerator and microwave. I grabbed a can of ginger ale from the fridge and sat at my desk and read the fax.

Justine Taborda, a Colombian/American, woke up one morning two weeks ago with chest pains. Thinking it heartburn, she went to work at her office in Vancortland where she worked as a dental receptionist.

Around ten am, she collapsed and never regained consciousness. She died in Saint Joseph's Hospital two hours later. An autopsy revealed the defective valve in her heart that caused the massive heart attack that killed her.

Two days after the autopsy, he body was scheduled to be transported to the funeral home on Jerome Avenue when it was discovered missing.

Jane entered the basement and sat on the edge of my desk. I handed her the fax. She read it quickly. "Lovely," she said.

"I'm going to New York in the morning," I said.

"Why can't you ever have a case that takes you to Palm Beach, so I can tag along as your assistant?" Jane said.

"The next headless woman kidnapping case I get will be somewhere exotic, I promise," I said.

"You sweet talker you," Jane said.

"Jane, come help with the dumplings," Regan called from the steps.

"Gotta go," Jane said, kissed me and dashed up the steps.

I called Lawrence on the landline.

"I just read the fax," I said. "At least we can put a name to the body and give closure to her family."

"There is a lid on it until we get there," Lawrence said.

"I'll take a cab from the airport and meet you at the hospital," I said.

"Pack an overnight bag," Lawrence said.

After hanging up, I went upstairs and found Regan and Jane making chicken dumplings in the kitchen.

"I'm going to New York tomorrow morning," I said. "I'll be gone two days."

I saw the look of disappointment on Regan's face, but she nodded and said, "Okay, Dad."

"Where is Wally?" I said.

"Living room," Regan said.

Wally was working on something on his laptop. He was on the sofa. Molly was on his lap. Cuddles was sleeping beside him.

"Wally, a moment," I said.

He looked up at me.

"I just got conformation that the woman we found in unit 88 is not Barbara," I said.

Wally closed his eyes for a moment, Then he opened them and said, "Thank God she's still alive."

I didn't bother to explain things to him, he wasn't ready for the truth. "I'm going to New York tomorrow to get details," I said. "Are you ready to go home or do you need more time?"

"I don't want to be alone right now," Wally said.

"Good enough. Stay put," I said. "Now I'm going to grab a shower before dinner."

*   *   *

After dinner, Jane and I took coffee in the backyard. The moon was up, the stars were out and the breeze was soft.

"Those dumplings were perfect," I said.

"My mother's recipe," Jane said.

I sipped coffee and looked at the stars.

"Hey, Bekker, something I'm considering I want your thoughts on," Jane said.

She only calls me Bekker when it's serious. "I'm listening," I said.

"We talked about me retiring before, but this time I'm seriously considering it," Jane said. She paused and drank some coffee.

"And?" I said.

"Twenty-five years is enough," she said. "But the thing is I'm not sure if I'm retiring because I've had enough, or because I want us to get married."

"Why can't it be both?" I said.

"It can, I suppose," Jane said. "Thing is I don't want to make any mistakes here. I'm divorced once, I want us to last."

"What makes you think we won't?" I said.

"I know me, Jack," Jane said. "If I don't have something to do, I get antsy. Real antsy. Then I get bitchy. I don't want to lose you because I turn into Meryl Streep in *The Devil Wears Prada*."

"I won't pretend to know what that is," I said. "Retire or don't, I'll take you either way."

"I guess I have some thinking to do," Jane said.

"Don't take too long," I said. "I'm not a spring chicken anymore."

"That makes too of us," Jane said.

"We'll talk about it again when I get back," I said.

"Want me to stay over?" Jane said. "Keep an eye on things. I can sleep in the basement."

"I don't think Wally is going to do anything, but Regan would love the company," I said.

"I have two uniforms and a suitcase in the car," Jane said. "I can bunk on the couch tonight."

"If you get lonely, I'm a flight of stairs away," I said.

# Chapter Twenty-one

The red-eye flight got me into Kennedy Airport at ten-thirty in the morning. My carry-on held everything I needed for a two-day layover.

Kennedy is in Queens, Saint Joseph's Hospital is in the Bronx, the cab ride was long and uneventful.

Paul Lawrence was already there when I arrived, standing in front of the main entrance of the very large hospital.

"I came in late last night," Lawrence said. "I got us rooms at the Hilton in White Plains. Toss your bag in my rental."

Lawrence had rented a Toyota sedan. I tossed my bag onto the back seat.

"I called ahead," Lawrence said. "We're seeing the hospital administrator and the ME in charge of the morgue."

*　*　*

"I've been the administrator here for fifteen years and nothing like this has every happened before," the administrator said.

"I've been here twenty and never has something like this happened," the ME said.

"You've done as I asked and not notified the girl's family?" Lawrence said.

"Not a word to anybody," the administrator said.

91

"We'll take care of that ourselves," Lawrence said. "Can we see the morgue?"

The ME nodded. "Follow me," he said.

*   *   *

I'd been in morgues before. As a homicide detective, it was part of the job. The morgue at Saint Joseph's Hospital was the largest, nicest one I'd come across. It glistened from antiseptic and had twenty-four trays for bodies. Even the stainless steel operating table looked as if they'd been freshly polished.

"Which tray was Miss Taborda in?" Lawrence said.

"Twelve," the ME said.

"Who did the autopsy on her?" Lawrence said.

"I did," the ME said.

I looked at the door that lead to a hallway to the hospital.

"Who assisted you?" Lawrence said.

"My regular two surgeons," the ME said.

I looked at a second door on the opposite side of the room.

"How many people have access to the morgue?" Lawrence said.

"Myself, my two regular surgeons, the orderlies assigned and the cleaning crew," the ME said.

"The only camera in here is the one for the operating table," Lawrence said. "Correct?"

"We've always respected the deceased," the ME said.

I walked to the second door. It was locked with an emergency exit arm that;. in case of emergency it could be pushed to open the door.

"Is this door alarmed?" I said.

"If you push the bar," the ME said.

"Can you disarm it for me?" I said.

The ME fished out a set of keys and disarmed the alarm on the emergency exit bar. I pushed open the door and we walked out to a private bay away from the emergency room.

"Privacy is utmost in our mind when transporting a..." the ME said.

"Dead body," I said.

"Yes," the ME said.

Mounded beside the door was an intercom system. Above the door was a mounted CCTV camera.

"Where does that feed to?" I said.

"The main security room I suppose," the ME said.

"How long after the autopsy did you discover Miss Taborda missing?" I said.

"I did the autopsy on Wednesday and discovered the body missing on Friday," the ME said.

"Before we talk to security, we want to take a look at the before autopsy photographs," I said.

"Sure," the ME said.

Justine Taborda was a pretty redhead in life, with fine features and a mole just above her left breast.

We kept a head shot to show her parents.

\* \* \*

Ralph Brooker was a thirty year veteran of the NYPD, who retired as a lieutenant in the 42 in the Bronx. He worked a lot of tough neighborhoods in Queens, Brooklyn and the Bronx before retiring five years ago.

"I've been here three years now and this place is worse than The South Bronx back in the sixties," Brooker said. "Knifings, gunshot wounds every Saturday night in the EM. Drug overdoses most nights and several times there were stabbings right in the Emergency room. But never have we lost a body, at least on my watch."

"How many cameras in the hospital and grounds?" I said.

"One hundred and twenty-four," Brooker said. "Including the two parking garages."

"We'd like to see the video of the cameras in the hallway to the morgue and outside the morgue in the bay," I said.

"Don't you think I've looked at those a hundred times already," Brooker said.

"Let's make it a hundred and one," Lawrence said.

We watched the window from Wednesday to Friday several times. We watched the ME and his crew come and go a dozen times in the two day span. Three times the emergency bay door opened for a body to be removed, none of which were Miss Taborda.

"Run it back again," I said.

We watched it again, running it at high speed when there was no activity and slowing it down when there was activity.

Then I saw something that made my ears burn and my vision narrow.

The janitor.

He pushed a cleaning cart like the carts maids use in hotels. The cart was full of plastic garbage bags. A tray was filled with cleaning supplies. He wore latex gloves. His head was down, away from the camera.

The hallway was dark. The black and white recording was grainy.

"Hold it here," I said.

Brooker froze the recording as the maintenance man was about to unlock the door to the morgue with a set of keys.

"Note the time," I said.

"Eleven forty-seven on Thursday night," Lawrence said.

"Roll it," I said.

The maintenance man entered the morgue and was inside for nine minutes before he exited at eleven fifty-six and wheeled his cart along the hallway.

"Freeze it," I said.

Brooker froze the recording.

"Nine minutes to wipe everything down, empty the trash and clean two bathrooms, I don't think so," I said.

"Can you track that maintenance man?" Lawrence said.

"Camera to camera, it would take some doing," Brooker said.

"Get it done," Lawrence said.

"Before you do, keep rolling," I said.

At twelve fifty-one, another maintenance man showed up, entered the morgue with a set of keys and was inside for forty-three minutes before exiting.

"Get the ME over here right away," I said.

\* \* \*

We showed the ME the twelve-thirty-one part first. "That's Jerry McNeal, our regular maintenance man," he said.

Then we showed him the eleven-forty-seven part. "Who the blazes is that?" he said.

"That," I said. "Is your body snatcher."

Brooker looked at me.

"Nine minutes is plenty of time to go in, open tray number twelve, put the body in the cart and wheel her out into the night," I said.

"Jesus Christ," the ME said.

"Brooker, follow that first man," Lawrence said. "I don't care how long it takes, but find where he goes."

\* \* \*

Lawrence and I grabbed a burger and a cup of coffee in the hospital cafeteria.

"The body snatcher, whoever he is, is likely an employee or ex-employee of the hospital," Lawrence said. "He knows the hospital well and when it is staffed the least, the graveyard shift. He's either the kidnapper who wrote the note or is working with him."

"My money is on a three-way split," I said. "This whole thing took a lot of planning and a lot of time."

"How long was Bubbles with Wally?" Lawrence said.

"Three months," I said. "But they probably had the whole thing worked out well in advance and were waiting on just the right body."

"And along comes Justine Taborda," Lawrence said.

"And while stealing a dead body is a crime, it isn't murder and kidnapping," I said.

"What bothers me is this Bubbles," Lawrence said. "Everything about her seems to be conjured up out of thin air. The only real thing about her according to he fellow strippers is that she's a natural redhead."

"Which made Taborda the perfect choice," I said.

A security guard entered the cafeteria and came to the table. "Mr. Brooker wants to see you," he said.

\* \* \*

"One hundred and twenty-four cameras and twenty-four monitoring screens," Brooker said. "That means in order to cover all one hundred and twenty-four cameras the images have to change every five point one seconds."

We looked at the twenty-four monitors. Every five seconds they changed locations.

"On the graveyard shift when there are just four guards patrolling the entire hospital, one in the shack outside emergency and one watching monitors, the odds of catching this in real time were slim," Brooker said.

Brooker played a section of take he had spliced together. We watched the body snatcher enter the morgue at eleven forty-seven and exit nine minutes later. He pushed the cart down several dark hallways and entered a bathroom in a deserted hallway. He emerged from the bathroom after changing his clothes, donning a wig and dark glasses and pushing the body of Justine Taborda in a wheelchair. He dressed her in a trench coat, shoes, hat and dark glasses and she appeared to be sleeping. He pushed the wheelchair along a hallway and then to a connecting walkway that led directly to a parking garage. After that, we lost him.

"Right under our noses," Brooker said.

"Why nothing in the garage?" I said.

"There is an elevator that goes directly to the street," Brooker said. "He probably got on that."

"And right into a waiting car," Lawrence said.

"That's my guess," Brooker said.

"Burn me a copy of that," Lawrence said. "We might be able to face-recognize this asshole."

"Where is Yonkers from here?" I said.

"Turn right at the main entrance and walk ten blocks," Brooker said.

# Chapter Twenty-two

The drive to the home Jennifer Taborda shared with her parents was just eight blocks away from the hospital.

The Tabordas were not thrilled to see us, to say the least. They sat quietly in the living room and listened to Lawrence as he told them of her daughter's fate.

Mrs. Taborda cried the entire time.

"What kind of hospital is this they lose patients who died there?" Mr. Taborda said. He spoke with a thick, Colombian accent and it was difficult to understand him.

"It's not the hospital, Mr. Taborda," Lawrence said. "It's the criminals who used the hospital and your daughter for their kidnapping plan."

"We didn't know about the bad heart," Mrs. Taborda cried. "We would have taken her to a doctor had we known."

"She was otherwise healthy," Lawrence said. "There was no way you could have known."

"Our daughter will be returned to us?" Mrs. Taborda said.

"In the condition the body is in that might not be wise," I said.

"We can have her cremated and shipped to you," Lawrence said. "At our expense."

"Alright," Mr. Taborda said. "For our family that would be best."

* * *

We had dinner at the hotel.

"Do you really think you can get face recognition off that grainy, dark tape?" I said.

"No, but I have to try," Lawrence said. "There is always luck."

"Every damn person in that hospital needs to be interviewed," I said.

"I'll have six agents report tomorrow," Lawrence said. "Between them and us we'll speak to every person who worked that Thursday day and night."

"I'd like to see Robert Sample in the morning before we leave for the hospital," I said. "I'd like him to have his personal department screen every employee and see if any of them ever worked in a hospital."

"I should have thought of that one myself," Lawrence said.

"Let's order some dessert," I said.

* * *

I called home from my room. Regan answered the phone.

"Hey, Dad," she said. "Thanks for letting Jane babysit us. We had a good time today."

"What did you do?" I said.

"We took Wally to the mall for a makeover."

"What?"

"Haircut, his beard trimmed, new glasses and a whole new wardrobe," Regan said.

"Really? And he stood still for that?"

"Jane say, Wally do."

"How does he look?" I said.

"Like a well-groomed Weeble," Regan said. "Want to say hi to Jane?"

"Sure."

"Hey, Jack," Jane said when she came on the line.

"I understand today was Wally makeover day," I said.

"The little fuzzball actually looks human," Jane said. "Sort of."

"I probably won't be back until day after tomorrow," I said. "We have a lot to do. I'll fill you in when I get home."

"I'm working tomorrow, but I'll stay over again tomorrow night. I gotta go. It's my turn to play Wally."

After hanging up with Jane, I took a long, hot shower. Then I tossed on a T-shirt and shorts, grabbed a ginger ale from the mini-fridge and drank it while looking out the window.

Something about the whole thing was too perfect, too slick. It was planned well in advance and they waited for the right time and the right girl to fall in their lap to execute their plan.

Barbara worked at the Cupid's Retreat for a year. She couldn't have been planning it for that long. She was recruited.

By whom?

And when?

And why the identity of Barbara Bouchette.

Why Pittsburgh?

I picked up the phone and called Lawrence's room.

"Before we see Robert Sample, call your guys in D.C.," I said. "Have them check their database here and with Interpol for kidnappings with a similar MO. This isn't a first timer we're dealing with."

There was a long pause on the line. Then Lawrence said, "Damn, Jack, does that brain of yours have an off switch?"

"See you for breakfast," I said.

# Chapter Twenty-three

After an early breakfast, we drove to the Sample building to see Robert Sample. He was in his office.

"I'm surprised to see you back so soon," he said.

"We need you to do something for us," I said.

"If I can," Robert said.

"We need you to have your personnel department go through your files and check all employees for the past ten years who worked at hospitals, funeral homes and morgues."

"Good God," Robert said.

"We'll be here until tomorrow," Lawrence said. "We can stop back later this afternoon."

Robert nodded. "Alright," he said.

\* \* \*

Before we entered the hospital, Lawrence called his office in Washington and told his staff to check for similar kidnapping MOs in the data bank and Interpol.

Then we spent the next three hours in Brooker's office interviewing his security staff and parking attendants. Six of Lawrence's agents in various offices helped lighten the load.

We broke for lunch at one, ate in the hospital cafeteria and spent the afternoon interviewing orderlies, nurses, doctors and receptionists.

By five o'clock we exhausted the number of people we needed to talk to and left the hospital empty-handed.

On the drive back to White Plains, Lawrence called Robert and told him we were on the way to his office.

Traffic was heavy and we crawled to the FDR and north to Westchester and finally into White Plains.

It was after six pm by the time we entered Robert's office.

"Well, it took my people all day to check records, but we found three that worked in hospitals and one that drove a car for a funeral parlor," Robert said. "The records go back three to six years and none of them work here any longer."

"We'll need their contact information," Lawrence said.

"The folder on my desk," Robert said.

"Thanks, Robert," I said.

\* \* \*

We looked over the names over dinner.

Two of the four were women that worked as nurse's aids in hospitals. One in a hospital in Yonkers, the other in the Bronx. Of the two men, one was an orderly in a Manhattan hospital and the other drove a car for a funeral home in Queens.

"I can have the regional office run these four down," Lawrence said. "I need to get back to Washington. I can detour and give you a ride home if you want."

"Why not?" I said.

"I'll tell the pilot after dinner," Lawrence said.

\* \* \*

I called home from my room. Regan answered the phone.

"Hey, Dad," she said.

"I'm coming home tomorrow," I said. "Should be there around noon."

"We'll have lunch for you," Regan said. "Want to talk to Jane?"

"Sure."

After a short pause, Jane said, "That little son of a bitch beats me every time. I don't know how he does it, the friggin' Weeble."

"He's a genius," I said.

"A genius with two different colored socks on," Jane said.

"I thought you bought him new clothes," I said.

"We did."

"I'll be back around noon tomorrow," I said.

"I'll stay an extra night," Jane said. "Maybe a midnight rendezvous to the basement is in order."

"Maybe," I said.

After hanging up with Jane, I grabbed a ginger ale from the mini fridge and paced the room.

Four Sample employees worked in an industry that involved dead bodies.

Two were women, so it couldn't have been them in the hospital video. The FBI had yet to match the man in the video with face recognition, so who knows?

I picked up the phone and called Lawrence's room.

"Let me guess, you're pacing the room again," he said.

"The bearer bonds," I said.

"What about them?" Lawrence said.

"They're no good unless they're deposited into a bank or exchanged for cash," I said. "Can the FBI search for large deposits or exchanges of bearer bonds in the last two weeks? It's probably too soon, but if you red flag the system to give an alert if and when."

"You never stop thinking, do you, Jack?" Lawrence said.

"It's a curse."

"I'll do it in the morning," Lawrence said.

After hanging up, I flopped into bed and stared at the ceiling and waited to fall asleep.

# Chapter Twenty-four

"The New York regional office will run down the four Sample employees," Lawrence said. "D.C. will handle the bearer bonds."

"Ever have the feeling you missed something?" I said.

"Every day for the past twenty-five years," Lawrence said. "We got an hour to go, want some coffee?"

Lawrence brewed a pot in the galley. We drank cups and looked out the window and watched the clouds roll by for lack of anything better to do.

The pilot told us to buckle up and we felt the landing gear descend.

"Why Pittsburgh?" I said.

"Why not Pittsburgh?" Lawrence said.

"In that case, why not Cleveland or Denver or Saint Louis?" I said.

"Maybe she needed a place she figured no one would look for her and Pittsburgh popped into her mind?" Lawrence said.

"Her fake Social Security number is out of Pennsylvania," I said. "Last time I looked at a map, Pittsburgh was in Pennsylvania."

Lawrence sipped coffee as he stared at me.

"God, you're relentless," he said.

"Just because it isn't issued now doesn't mean it never was issued," I said.

"I'll add it to the list," Lawrence said.

"We're landing now," I said.

\* \* \*

I retrieved my car from long term parking and drove home. Regan and Wally were playing Frisbee in the backyard, Oz was reading a book in his easy chair.

"How'd it go?" Oz said when I flopped on the sofa.

"A lot of ifs and maybes but no definites" I said.

"A lot of that going around these days," Oz said.

"Jane working?" I said.

"She be back around six," Oz said. He closed his book. "When you going to marry that woman?"

"When the time is right," I said.

"No time like the present," Oz said.

"Hey, Dad," Regan said as she and Wally entered the living room.

"Hi, honey," I said. "Wally, look at you. Haircut, beard trimmed, new glasses, you look a lot better."

"They made me do it. The women," Wally said, "or they wouldn't feed me."

"Speaking of feeding, want some lunch?" Regan said.

"I think I'll grab a workout first," I said. "I'm kind of stiff from all the sitting."

"That called middle age," Oz said. "Just wait, it get over time."

I changed into sweats and did an hour in the backyard. About thirty minutes with weights and a solid thirty minutes on the heavy bag.

I didn't count reps. My mind was working overtime and by the time I sat down for lunch, I had reached a conclusion.

"Wally, I said as I bit into a thick turkey sandwich. "Tomorrow we take a road trip to see an old friend."

"Who?" Wally said.

"Do you remember Frank Kagan?" I said.

"The lawyer?"

"That's the one," I said. "We'll leave after breakfast."

"Dad, I have to work at the pet store," Regan said.

"We won't be long," I said. "I'm thinking we should go out to dinner tomorrow night."

"I love Taco Bell," Wally said.

"As tempting as that sounds, I was thinking more of a family place," I said.

"Other day I went to the post office, there's a new Greek place just opened," Oz said.

"It's just a few blocks from the pet store," Regan said.

"Sounds good," I said. "After lunch, let's go for a run on the beach."

Oz, Regan and Wally stared at me.

"I'll go for a run, you can play with the dog," I said.

\* \* \*

While Oz sat in a chair and read a book, Regan and Wally played Frisbee by the water with Cuddles.

The run wasn't for my body, it was for my mind.

After a certain point, when your body found the zone, your mind cleared and thoughts became crystal clear. I solved many a crime while putting the pieces together during a long run.

Six miles to and fro, and by the time I dumped myself into a folding chair beside Oz, Regan and Wally were on blankets with Cuddles.

Regan handed me a bottle of water.

"Thanks, honey," I said.

"Mr. Bekker, what do we need to see the lawyer for?" Wally said. "I was just wondering."

"Frank Kagan has become a friend and a valuable ally," I said.

Oz looked at me. "We talking bout the mob lawyer?" he said.

"Let's go home and get ready for dinner," I said.

* * *

While we waited for Jane to change out of her uniform, I called Lawrence from the hard line phone on my desk.

"So far no movement on the bearer bonds," Lawrence said. "Of course we've only just scratched the surface."

"What about the Social Security number?" I said.

"It was issued to a Jennifer Pennock," Lawrence said. "She died ten years ago in a car accident in York, Pennsylvania. Her SS number was returned and never reissued."

"So how did Bubbles come by it?" I said.

"No clue at the present time," Lawrence said.

"Thanks, Paul," I said.

I went upstairs and met Jane in the living room. She had changed out of her uniform and replaced it with designer jeans, a white blouse and three-inch heels that bumped her up to almost six-feet-tall.

Jane took Wally's arm. "Shall we go?" she said.

Oz took Regan's arm. "We shall," Oz said.

Lacking an arm to link, I followed.

# Chapter Twenty-five

Frank Kagan listened carefully for about twenty minutes while I spoke. He served coffee for me and hot chocolate for Wally.

When I finished talking, he said, "Why on earth would I hire you to investigate a kidnapping that took place in New York? The Sample family must have a team of lawyers at their disposal."

"Appearances," I said.

"Whose?" Kagan said.

"Mine."

Kagan looked at Wally. "Is this okay with you?" he said.

"Is what okay?" Wally said.

Kagan sighed. "Never mind," he said.

"Oh, you mean hiring Mr. Bekker, is that what you mean?" Wally said.

"Officially I am working for Wally," I said. "Pro Bono."

"Because if that's what you mean I'm okay with it," Wally said.

"And it will be Pro Bono with me as well," Kagan said.

"That is what you mean, isn't it?" Wally said.

"This isn't about money, Frank," I said. "Now will you hire me or not?"

Kagan nodded. "Nut the next time I do need you, you really will work Pro Bono. I'll have my receptionist draw up a letter of employment."

"Thanks, Frank," I said.

"No go wait out in the reception area, I have work to do," Kagan said.

"What's going on?" Wally said.

"I'll explain it to you later," I said.

\*　\*　\*

After dinner, Jane and I took coffee in the backyard. I told her about Kagan and what I planned to do.

"That brain of yours is sharper than ever," Jane said and flared her nostrils.

Whenever Jane flairs her nostrils, trouble is right around a corner. Like a bull being teased with a red cape, the charge was inevitable.

"What?" I said.

"Don't what me, Bekker," Jane said.

"Usually I have a hard time following you once you've lost your temper, but this time I'm lost," I said.

"Who lost their… sometimes you are such a world-class numb-scull, it's beyond belief," Jane said.

She lit a cigarette, inhaled and exhaled through her nose looking like a blonde, exotic dragon.

"Are we speaking in some kind of female code I don't know about?" I said.

"Don't you dare go down that road with me, not after all the shit we've been through together," Jane said.

She handed me the cigarette and I took a puff.

"Don't let Regan see you," she said.

I returned the cigarette. "Maybe if you explain it to me real slow so my male brain can comprehend what I did wrong I'll understand," I said.

"If I retire and we get married, I know you're not going to retire and I'll be left behind with nothing to do," Jane said. "I've seen it happen, Jack. Cops retire and then they shrivel up on the vine and die."

"You got all this from the word 'what'?" I said.

"I'm serious," Jane said.

"My pension and benefits are decent enough and the money I earn from private work is excellent," I said. "Your pension and benefits will be likewise. Ever see my business card?"

"Sure. I have some," Jane said.

"It says John Bekker, licensed private investigator," I said. "I see no reason why it can't say Bekker and Bekker, licensed private investigators, can you?"

"Not a bad idea," Jane said. "With my brains and your brawn we could—"

"My brawn?" I said.

"Don't interrupt," Jane said.

The kitchen door slid open. "Dessert and coffee," Regan said. "I smell smoke. Dad, you better not be smoking. Jane?"

"It's me," Jane said. "Guilty."

"Am I going to have to work on you, too?" Regan said.

\* \* \*

Sometime after midnight, Jane crept down to the basement. A nightlight gave off just enough light for her to navigate to the day bed.

"Move over," she said.

I lifted the covers and made room.

"Start your engine, Jack," Jane said. "Mine's already in gear."

# Chapter Twenty-six

"I'm going to Pittsburgh tomorrow," I said.

"What for?" Walt said. "Nobody goes to Pittsburgh unless they have to and even then they don't want to."

"I have to," I said. "I need a favor first."

"That explains the dozen donuts from Pat's," Walt said.

"I would have brought those anyway," I said. "I figured the favor would cost me lunch."

"Tell me what you need over a thick, juicy burger," Walt said.

I drove us to a diner near the police station and we ordered the bacon burger specials.

"Ten years ago a young woman named Jennifer Pennock died in a car accident in York, Pennsylvania," I said. "See what you can find out about it from the police reports."

"Does this have anything to do with Wally?" Walt said.

"Possibly," I said. "It might be connected. Somehow."

"Somehow?" Walt said.

"How long could it take to dig up some old police reports on a car accident?" I said.

"This lunch is on you, right?" Walt said.

"You know it is," I said.

"Throw in dessert and I'll see what I can do," Walt said.

*　*　*

I spent the afternoon working out in the backyard. Jump rope to warm up, a good session with the weights, push-ups, pull-ups, then the heavy bag and speed bag.

I didn't count sets or reps. I kept my mind clear and concentrated on my thought process surrounding Wally's would-be missing fiancé.

Wally meets stripper at the bachelor party.

Supposedly she was hired from a random phone call to the Cupid's Retreat strip club in Queens, New York. Supposedly.

Wally and Bubbles fall in love. Supposedly.

Bubbles quits stripping and moves into an apartment provided by Wally until they get married. Supposedly.

Bubbles is then kidnapped. Supposedly. The ransom is fifteen million in bearer bonds.

The ransom buys the headless, handless remains of Justine Taborda, who died of natural causes a week or so before the kidnapping occurred.

The I-9 information for Bubbles, including her name is completely false.

Same for her college records.

The Social Security number given by Bubbles belonged to a girl who died in a car accident in York, PA a decade earlier. Jennifer Pennock.

The only Bouchette registered at the college was a woman who graduated thirty years ago. Laura Bouchette and she would be in her fifties by now and no one would mistake her for Bubbles.

How long did it take to plan the entire thing?

Bubbles was with Wally for three months.

That was long enough, especially if you had the idea stewing longer than that.

Workout over, I went for a shower. By the time I slipped into a clean warm-up suit, Regan had returned from her job at the pet store.

I grabbed a can of ginger ale and joined her, Wally and Oz in the living room.

"I'm going to Pennsylvania tomorrow," I said.

"Not again," Regan said.

"Overnight, I promise," I said.

"Dad, I… never mind," Regan said. "Come on, Wally, let's go to the backyard."

Regan Wally, Cuddles and Molly went to the kitchen and entered the backyard.

I took a seat on the sofa. "She's upset I'm going away," I said.

"It's not that," Oz said.

"Then what?" I said.

"She going to be twenty in a few months," Oz said. "She work a part time job and starts her second year in college come fall. She's come a long way, a very long way."

"Don't you think I know that better than anybody," I said.

"Do you?" Oz said.

"What are you trying to say?" I said.

"Boy at work, he asked her for a date," Oz said. "I met him in the store about a week ago. He's her age, goes to college and still has pimples. She don't know what to do. She need advice."

"I see," I said. "I should talk to her then."

"God you dense sometimes," Oz said. "She need woman-to-woman talk, something you can't give her."

"I should—" I said.

"Call Jane, yeah," Oz said.

I went to my basement office and called Jane. She was in her office. I explained the situation to her.

"I'll be there by seven," she said.

"Thank you," I said.

"Thank me around midnight," Jane said.

After hanging up with Jane, Walt called a bit later on my cell.

"Still have a fax machine?" he said.

"Of course," I said.

"I'm faxing you the police and insurance reports from the accident," Walt said.

"Thank you," I said.

"Ah, humility," Walt said.

"I'll have a dozen donuts sent to the squad room," I said.

"I'm partial to chocolate," Walt said.

"I know."

I hung up and waited for the fax. It came as I was finishing the ginger ale.

Jennifer Pennock was seventeen-years-old when a car accident took her life. She was a passenger in a car driven by her older brother, Josh, who was nineteen. He also died in the accident. It was December and the road was slick from freezing rain. Jennifer had applied to Penn State York University for fall enrollment and was visiting the campus during Christmas break. They were driving home on the Pennsylvania Turnpike when a tractor trailer lost control and slammed into the car driven by Josh, killing him and Jennifer instantly.

Laura Pennock and he husband Michael and their youngest daughter Lauren, fourteen at the time, buried Josh and Jennifer at a cemetery in Pittsburgh.

It was a tragic and pointless accident that claimed two young lives and may have nothing to do with Wally and Bubbles.

But then again.

I went to my room and packed a bag for the trip. Then I went to the backyard. "Guys, Jane is coming for dinner, what should we do, cook or order out?"

"Taco Bell," Wally said.

"Pizza," Regan said.

"I go with pizza," I said. "Let's check with Oz."

We went to the living room and asked Oz.

"Sorry, butterball, I gotta go with pizza," Oz said.

I called the pizza place in town and ordered three large pies, one with extra everything, one with sausage and broccoli and one regular and a dozen garlic rolls. I asked for a seven-thirty delivery.

Regan and Wally returned to the backyard with Cuddles.

I went back to my office.

Oz stayed in his chair with his book.

Jane arrived at seven and Oz let her in and then called me.

"Regan's in the backyard," I said to Jane.

"Take Wally off my hands," Jane said.

Wally came in, Jane went out, Oz said, "Be smart once in your life and ask her no questions."

\* \* \*

Jane snuck down to the basement around midnight. "Move over," she said as she got into the daybed.

"How did it go, your talk with Regan?" I said.

"Girl talk, Jack," Jane said.

"I know that," I said. "About what?"

"About things father's don't want to know about their little girls," Jane said.

I stared up at the dark ceiling.

"Uh oh," Jane said. "I think I just shut off your motor. Let's see if I can find the restart button."

# Chapter Twenty-seven

The plane ride to Pittsburgh was smooth and uneventful. The red-eye flight got me to Pittsburgh International at ten-thirty am. While most passengers played with their cell phones and laptops, I read a paperback book.

Before leaving home, I did some online searching and after renting a car at the airport, I entered the address for the hall of records into the GPS unit.

The drive, with traffic, took about forty-five minutes. I parked in a municipal lot, grabbed a large coffee from a deli and entered the large building.

I went to the marriage license record division. I had to wait for a computer to free up and then sat down to work.

It took a while to find it, but there it was.

Laura Bouchette married Michael Pennock in 1992 in Pittsburgh. I printed a copy and then went to the Registry of Deeds.

That search took even longer, but finally I located the purchase of a home by Michael and Laura Pennock.

After that, I checked tax records and they still paid taxes on the home they purchased nearly three decades ago.

After printing up what I needed, I left the building, found a coffee shop and grabbed a late lunch.

Then I drove around for a while until I settled on a motel off the interstate and checked in for one night.

I killed time with a ginger ale and a newspaper, then at five o'clock, I programed the GPS in the rental car and drove to the home of Laura and Michael Pennock.

They lived in a nice suburb of Pittsburgh on a tree lined street. The front lawn was freshly mowed and a large flowerbed was the centerpiece.

There was a two-car garage and a car was parked in the driveway.

I parked behind the car and walked to the front door and rang the bell.

A pretty woman with dark hair and blue eyes answered the door. "Yes?" she said.

"You must be Lauren," I said.

"Do I know you?" Lauren said.

I had my identification at the ready and showed it to her.

"A private investigator?" Lauren said.

"I'm here to speak to your parents," I said. "It's very important."

"Wait here," Lauren said.

She closed the door and when it opened again, Michael Pennock looked at me. "My daughter says you're a private investigator."

I showed him my identification.

"Well, what is it you want?" Michael said.

"A few minutes of your time," I said.

\*   \*   \*

We sat at the kitchen table,

"We finished dinner an hour ago, but the coffee is fresh," Laura said.

After Laura filled cups for me, Michael, herself and Lauren, she sat beside her husband.

"So what is this about?" Michael said.

"Have you ever heard of Sample Iced Tea?" I said.

"Sure," Laura said. "We have some in the fridge."

"Well, a few weeks ago, one of the principal owners of Sample Iced Tea had his fiancé kidnapped and the ransom was fifteen million," I said.

"That's terrible but what does that have to do with us?" Michael said.

"The kidnapped woman identified herself as Barbara Bouchette," I said.

"What?" Laura said.

"She used a Social Security number that belonged to your daughter Jennifer and she also claimed to attend the College of Westchester," I said.

"Our Jennifer?" Laura said.

"Is this some kind of sick joke?" Michael said.

"No it isn't," I said. "I'm going to show you a photograph of the kidnapped woman, alright?"

"Go ahead," Michael said.

I showed them the photograph of Wally and Bubbles.

Lauren gasped and said, "That's Barbara Wilcox."

"My God I think you're right," Michael said. "She dyed her hair and she's older but I think it's her."

"Who is Barbara Wilcox?" I said.

"Jennifer's best friend in high school," Lauren said. "They were as tight as sisters. She took the accident hard, real hard."

"Barbara would sleep here and Jen over at her house," Laura said. "They even worked together at the same store at the mall. They were thick as thieves those two."

"After Jennifer died, she got into drugs, dropped out of high school in her senior year and ran away," Michael said.

"Her parents were devastated I'm afraid," Laura said. "They moved a few years after she ran off. I don't know where. They broke off all ties with everyone."

"Do you remember their names and where they lived?" I said.

"Sure," Lauren said. "I'll write it down for you."

"Did they get her back, Barbara I mean?" Michael said.

"Not yet," I said.

"Too bad," Michael said.

"Thank you for your time and information," I said. "I realize I brought back some bad memories."

"I hope they find her," Lauren said. "If and when thy do tell her we said hello."

\* \* \*

I drove back to motel, stopping first at a coffee shop for two burgers, fries and a ginger ale.

Thick as thieves. That's what Lauren Pennock called them.

If Barbara Wilcox and Jennifer Pennock were that close, it was possible Barbara knew Jennifer's Social Security number and where Laura went to college.

After Jennifer died, Barbara started doing drugs, dropped out of school and ran away from home and drifted east.

She winds up a stripper in New York. The money is good, sure, but she's twenty-eight now and it won't be long before you're no longer a headliner.

What do you do?

Become involved in an elaborate kidnapping scheme after hooking up with a billionaire genius too confused to wear matching socks and walk away fifteen million dollars richer.

There was no way Barbara Wilcox cooked up such a complicated kidnapping plan.

She was in it up to her eyeballs, but she didn't plan or execute it.

That part came from someone else.

The question was who?

I finished my burgers and fries and called home. Regan answered the call.

"Hey, Dad," she said.

"How's it going?" I said.

"Good. Jane had to work late so she won't be over," Regan said.

"I'll be home tomorrow afternoon," I said.

"I know," Regan said.

"Listen, this thing I'm helping Wally with, I'll probably have to take several more trips, okay?" I said.

"I know. It's okay."

"Thanks, honey. I'll see you tomorrow," I said.

After hanging up with Regan, I got into bed and thought for a while. What would I do, how would I react if I was the parent of Jennifer Pennock?

I already knew the answer to that. I crawled inside a bottle and stayed there for a decade and missed ten years of my daughter's life.

If I had to do it over again, what would I do?

How many have asked themselves that same question?

How many have lied to themselves about the answer?

I fell asleep thinking about Barbara Wilcox.

# Chapter Twenty-eight

I walked through my front door a bit after noon.

Oz was in his chair, reading a book. Wally and Regan were in the backyard with Cuddles. Molly was sleeping on Oz's lap.

"How it go?" Oz said.

"Good," I said. "I think I made some progress."

"But not enough."

"Not yet," I said. "Right now I want to talk to Regan for a moment."

"Be gentle."

I went to the backyard. "Regan, how about we go for a jog on the beach?" I said.

"Now?" Regan said.

"Two plane rides in twenty-four hours, I'm stiff as a board," I said. "And I could use the company."

Wally had a look of panic on his face. "I have a report to finish," he said.

"No problem, Wally," I said. "Regan, go change. I'll meet you in ten minutes."

\*   \*   \*

I parked in the municipal lot and we walked to the sand. It was crisp afternoon and the beach was deserted.

We started slow, barely above a jog.

"I've been thinking," I said.

"Uh oh," Regan said.

"I've missed a lot of your life, honey," I said. "I have no excuse for my actions except weakness."

"You, weak?" Regan said. "And slow down. I have to take two steps to your one."

"I can't get those years back, but we're together now and I want you to know I love you more than anything," I said.

"I know that, Dad," Regan said.

"I want you to know you can talk to me about anything," I said. "That I'm always here for you."

"What did Jane tell you?" Regan said.

"Jane would never violate a private conversation even if I asked her to," I said.

We were warmed up at that point and opened our stride a bit. At the one and a half mile mark, we stopped, sat in the sand and unclipped our water bottles from our hips and drank a bit.

"Dad, the job at the pet store has been good for me," Regan said. "I'm socializing with people and earning my own money. I'm not as shy anymore."

"You've come a long way in a couple of years," I said.

"The thing is, I spent most of my teen years at the hospital," Regan said. "I'm not sure how to act around boys. I'm almost twenty but I might as well be twelve."

"Is there a boy?" I said.

"His name is Anthony Bortone but everybody calls him Tony," Regan said. "We work the same shift together at the store. He's very shy like me and we talk a lot. The other day we talked about going on a date together."

"Well, going on a date together is more fun then going on a date separately," I said.

Regan shook her head at me. "You can't go on a date alone, Dad, even I know that," she said.

"That's not entirely true," I said. "In my day, if there was a high school dance and you chose to go alone we called it going stag."

"Stag? That sounds like some kind of cattle," Regan said.

"So about Tony, want my suggestion?" I said.

"Sure."

"Make plans but keep it simple," I said. "Dinner and a movie. Plan to go Dutch before you pick a day."

"Dutch?" Regan said.

"Something us old people used to do when we were your age," I said. "We agreed to each pay half for everything before we went on the date."

"He doesn't have a car," Regan said. "He walks to the pet store."

"But you do, so he pays for half the gas," I said.

"I'll talk to him about it at work tomorrow," Regan said.

"About the women stuff," I said.

"Jane covered that."

"Well, let's start running," I said.

\* \* \*

"Barbara Bouchette is really Barbara Wilcox, a friend of Jennifer Pennock and Jennifer's mother's maiden name was Bouchette and they are all from Pittsburgh," Jane said. "Barbara and Jennifer were best friends until Jennifer was killed in a car accident and then Barbara ran away from home and winds up Wally's stripper girlfriend who fakes her own kidnapping. Is that about it?"

"That's the abridged version," I said. "But yeah."

"You share this with your FBI guy or Walt?" Jane said.

"Not yet."

"Why not?"

"I want to poke around some more first," I said.

Jane wiggled around in the daybed until she was on top of me. "Speaking of poking," she whispered.

# Chapter Twenty-nine

I thought about my next move for twenty-four hours.

During that time, I worked out in the backyard, ran on the beach, grilled lunch for Oz and Wally, played Frisbee with Regan, Wally and Cuddles, watched a ballgame with Oz and let my thoughts fall where they may.

At dinner, I said, "I'm flying back to New York. Wally, since you're paying for my expenses I need you to approve."

With a mouthful of mashed potatoes, Wally said, "Approve what?"

"Paying expenses to New York," I said.

"Want me to get the jet to pick you up?" Wally said.

"Not necessary," I said.

"How long will you be gone?" Regan said.

"No more than two days," I said.

After dinner, I went to my office and called Jane and told her I would be in New York for at least two days.

"Want me to babysit the gang?" she said.

"If you wouldn't mind," I said.

"Be there after work tomorrow," she said.

After talking to Jane, I called the airlines and reserved a seat on the red-eye flight to New York.

* * *

Upon landing in Kennedy Airport, I rented a car and drove north to White Plains. Robert Sample was in his office and agreed to see me at eleven o'clock after a board meeting.

The entire Sample family, minus Wally, was at the boardroom table.

Robert was at the head of the table with Steven, Susan, Amy and Barbara spaced out on his left and right side.

"Get our money back yet?" Barbara said when I entered the boardroom.

"Barbara, give the man a chance to talk," Robert said.

"Yes, Barbara, shut up for once," Susan said. "I'd like to hear what Mr. Bekker has to say."

"Alright, Mr. Bekker, speak," Barbara said.

"Do I get a treat first?" I said. "Maybe you want me to roll over or give you my paw or do a trick for you."

"How dare you speak to—" Barbara said.

"Miss Sample, shut up," I said.

Barbara went red in the face, but before she could yell at me, Robert said, "Barbara, please be quiet. We'd like to know the reason for Mr. Bekker's visit."

"We haven't recovered the bearer bonds as yet," I said. "But the FBI is working on it. I have been officially retained by Wally to investigate separately from the FBI and Police."

"More money down the drain," Barbara said.

"I'm working Pro Bono, just expenses," I said.

"May I ask why?" Robert said.

"Wally is my friend," I said. "And I don't want to see him get hurt anymore than he already has."

"And when you tell him he was taken for a ride by his stripper hoe, what will you be doing then?" Barbara said.

"You have a big mouth, Barbara,' Susan said. "Why don't you try being quiet just one time?"

"He's going to get hurt, there is no doubt about that," I said. "But if I can catch them and return the bonds, I can minimize that hurt. That's what I came here to tell you."

Robert looked at me. "You know more than you're telling us," he said.

"Wally is my client," I said. "I owe him confidentially."

Robert nodded. "If there is anything you need," he said.

"I'll ask," I said.

* * *

I checked into the same hotel as previously in White Plains and drove the rental car to the Cupid's Retreat strip club in Queens.

The bouncer at the door remembered me and waved the fifteen-dollar fee.

"I'm here to see the owner," I told him.

He motioned to another bouncer who came to us.

"Take him to see the boss," he said.

"I thought I might see you again," the manager said.

"Why is that?" I said.

"You left here shall we say unfulfilled," the manager said. "Find anything on that I-9?"

"That's not why I'm here," I said. "I want to talk to your dancers again. I'm trying to figure out if Bubbles had one particular fan."

The manager stood up from behind his desk. "Let's go see the ladies," he said.

We walked to the green room where the manager said, "Ladies, a moment of your time is needed."

"I remember you," a stripper said. "You were asking questions about Barbara."

"That's right," I said. "And I'd like to ask a few more if you don't mind."

"What do you want to know this time?" a stripper said.

"Did she have one particular fan that stands out?" I said. "Somebody who tipped better, was always present when she did her shows, like that."

"You know who might know that, Jackie," a stripper said.

"And Jackie is?" I said.

"A headliner," the manager said. "She's on now."

I looked at the stripper. "Why do you think Jackie might know?" I said.

"They hung out together sometimes between shows," the stripper said.

"Can you ask her to come to the manager's office when she gets off?" I said.

"Sure."

The manager and I returned to his office where he sat behind his desk. "What's so important about all this anyway?" he said.

"It's classified," I said.

"Maybe you can tell me who actually shot Kennedy," the manager said.

There was a knock on the door, it opened and Jackie walked in. "You wanted to see me?" she said.

Gratefully she wore a robe over her lack of costume.

"This man has some questions for you," the manager said.

Jackie locked up at me. Even with her platform heels, she was a half foot shorter than me. "About what?" she said.

"Barbara Bouchette," I said.

"You were her a few weeks ago," Jackie said. "I was off that day. The girls told me about it."

"I'd like to ask you a few questions about Barbara," I said.

Jackie shrugged. "Go ahead," she said.

"She had a lot of fans here at the club," I said.

"Tons. She was really good. Better than me for sure," Jackie said.

"Anybody stick out?" I said. "Somebody you might recognize."

"Now that you mention it, there was one guy I used to see all the time at her shows," Jackie said. "I used to watch her from the balcony and try to pick up a few of her tricks. I'd see him every show and then he stopped coming."

"How long ago?" I said.

"Maybe five, six months ago," Jackie said. "It was before Barbara quit."

"Ever see them socialize together?" I said.

"That's not allowed in the club," Jackie said. "I can't speak for outside the club."

"Would you recognize him again if you saw him?"

"I think so, yeah."

"Okay, thank you," I said.

"That's it?" Jackie said.

"That's it," I said. "But I'll leave you my card in case you think of anything else."

*   *   *

I sat in my hotel room and thought, drinking cups of coffee and wishing I had a cigarette.

Every story ever written has a catalyst. Without it there would be no story to tell.

Good versus evil.

The good guy doesn't get the chance to be good without the bad guy.

Every novel, every play, every movie ever made has a catalyst. Something to set the story in motion.

John Wayne can't kill the bad guy if there isn't one.

Ten years ago, Barbara 'Bubbles' Bouchette is Barbara Wilcox, best friend to Jennifer Pennock. After Jennifer is killed in a car

130

accident, Barbara Wilcox runs away from home and assumes the last name of Laura Pennock's maiden name of Bouchette.

Fast forward and she's a headline stripper in a new York club.

She responds to a request for a private show at the Sample warehouse for a bachelor party. An accidental meeting or by design?

She strikes up a relationship with Wally. A chance meeting or by design?

She quits stripping and moves into an apartment paid for by Wally pending their marriage. The real thing or part of the plan?

Three months later, Bubbles is kidnapped. After the bonds are delivered, the body of Justine Taborda, minus head and hands is left in unit 88 to find. Justine died of natural cause a week or so before the kidnapping and was stolen from the hospital in the Bronx.

Barbara Wilcox and company ride off into the sunset some fifteen million dollars richer.

One thing was certain, Barbara Wilcox was not the catalyst.

So who was?

Somebody planned the entire thing.

Somebody had access to the hospital morgue.

The same somebody?

Or two different people.

The fan from the headliner act?

He stopped showing up and soon after Barbara quit stripping.

Every story needs a catalyst.

I called home and got Regan on the phone.

"Hey, Dad," Regan said. "It's set for Saturday."

"What is set for Saturday?" I said.

"My movie date with Tony," Regan said. "Do I need to ask you to be nice?"

"Nope. I'll just be myself," I said.

"Please be anything but that," Regan said. "Wait, Jane wants to talk to you."

"Be yourself and that poor kid will run home and lock himself in his room," Jane said. "Wait, Oz wants to talk to you."

"You scare that kid and Regan disown your dumb ass," Oz said.

"I haven't done anything," I said. "I'm not even there for Christ sake."

"That angry voice of yours will scare that kid out of a year's growth," Oz said.

"I wasn't angry until now," I said.

"Hold on," Oz said.

"Okay, Dad, we're making dinner now," Regan said. "See you tomorrow."

I hung up the phone. "What the hell did I do?" I said aloud.

After licking my wounds, I decided to eat in the hotel and pay twice for a burger than what it's worth.

The bonds hadn't turned up as yet. My guess is they were sitting in a bank safe deposit box somewhere until the heat died down and the investigation went cold.

A long time ago when I was heading up a task force on organized crime, I was given a piece of advice by the retiring commander.

He said, "The way to smoke these mobsters out is the same way you smoke bees out, with smoke so they can't breathe and have to come up for air."

It worked, too, but the collateral damage was my wife was killed and my daughter left traumatized.

Still, it might be worth a shot.

# Chapter Thirty

Regan was at her job at the pet store when I arrived home. Oz was reading a book in the backyard. Wally was working on his laptop in the living room.

I grabbed a ginger ale from the fridge and sat down on the sofa to talk to Wally.

"Wally, I want to talk to you," I said.

He looked up from his laptop.

"How much money do you have?" I said.

"Geeze, I don't know," Wally said. "Is that important?"

"I thinking of posting a reward for information on Bubbles and I want to make sure you can spare say ten million," I said.

"My salary is fifteen million a year with stock options and profit sharing," Wally said. "I made around sixty million last year. I think I'm worth around six hundred million or so."

"Would you be willing to post a reward for information on Barbara?" I said. "Ten million."

"I'd give it all to get her back," Wally said.

"Ten million should do," I said.

"How do we do it?" Wally said.

"I have to work out the details and I'll let you know," I said.

"Do you think it will work?" Wally said.

"Money makes rats out of everybody," I said.

I went to my office and called Lawrence in Washington.

Al Lamanda

"I was wondering what you've been up to," he said.

I told him about Barbara Wilcox, Laura Pennock, maiden name Bouchette and her daughter Jennifer.

"You got all that working by yourself?" Lawrence said.

"Sometimes you get lucky," I said.

"If that's luck, pick me six winning numbers," Lawrence said.

"There's more," I said and told him about Jackie.

"Except we have nothing to show her," Lawrence said.

"Not yet," I said. "Wally is going to offer a ten million dollar reward for information on Bubbles."

"All that's going to do is bring out the crazies," Lawrence said.

"True, but one out of a million and all that," I said.

"And how are you spreading the word and who will field the calls?" Lawrence said.

"The New York newspapers and I'll rig a number to call that goes directly to my answering machine so I can screen them," I said.

"And you'll give me any hot leads you come up with, right?" Lawrence said.

"Have I ever held out on you?" I said.

"Well, I can't stop you from doing this, but if you hold back on me no more free rides in the jet," Lawrence said.

"I'll call you when I have it figured out," I said.

After I changed into sweats, I went to the backyard. Oz was in a chair with Molly on his lap and with Cuddles sleeping beside the chair.

"She all excited about her date," Oz said. "Be a good dad and don't go berserk when he get here."

"I'm not—why does everybody think I'll go berserk?" I said. "I want her to heave a normal life and that includes dating boys."

"Remember that boy wanted to teach her surfing at the trailer?" Oz said. "He thought you were going to shoot him."

"That was two years ago," I said.

"That young deputy of Jane's, remember him?" Oz said.

"He was too old for her," I said.

"He wet his pants like a little baby," Oz said. "And then that nice looking boy from the—"

"I get your point," I said.

"Good," Oz said. He returned to his book.

I warmed up with the jump rope. Then some push-ups and pull-ups before moving over to the heavy bag and speed bag and ending with some weights.

During the workout I started composing the wording for the information reward. It had to be eye-catching and worded in such a way to make someone out there rat on a friend or even a colleague.

By the time my workout was finished, Oz had gone in the house.

I went inside and found Regan and Wally playing a video game.

"Hey, Dad," Regan said. "Jane will be here around seven."

"What should we do for dinner?" I said. "And no, Wally, not Taco Bell."

"Something on the grill?" Regan said.

"Good idea," I said. "I'll go change."

After a quick shower, I tossed on a clean warm-up suit and met Oz in the living room. "Let's head to town for some supplies," I said.

The first stop was the meat market for some chicken and steak tips. Then the grocery store for what-nots, including a crock of baked beans.

As we drove home, Oz said, "How much longer Wally be with us?"

"I'm not sure," I said. "We can ask him."

"Ask but don't push," Oz said. "We don't want him leaving the nest before he ready to fly again."

"It sounds to me like you've grown fond of him," I said.

"Nobody said that," Oz said. "I just don't want whatever befalls him on my conscience."

"You said that about me ten years ago," I said.

"And look how swell you turned out," Oz said.

* * *

I was heating up the grill when Jane arrived. She popped out to the backyard and greeted me with a kiss.

"What's for din-din?" she said.

"Chicken, steak tips, baked potatoes and baked beans," I said.

"Yummy," Jane said. "Well, I'll be in Regan's room having a heart-to-heart. Call us when it's ready."

Thirty minutes later, we sat at the backyard picnic table to eat.

As I cut into a steak tip, Regan said, "But Jane, what if I'm not comfortable doing that on a first date?"

I looked at Regan.

"It's expected, honey," Jane said.

"What?" I said. "What is expected?"

Oz looked at his watch. "Three seconds to red in the face," he said. "A new record. Pay up, Jane."

"Funny," I said.

"Hell yeah it is," Oz said.

* * *

Sometime after midnight, Jane snuck into the basement and got into the daybed.

"Have you come to show me what is expected?" I said.

"Only if you show me first," Jane said.

# Chapter Thirty-one

I worked on composing the reward ad for most of the morning. Jane had to work and Wally and Regan occupied their time first playing with Cuddles in the backyard and then by playing a video game.

Around one Oz and I made lunch. Turkey sandwiches on thick cut slice of crusty bread with chips and ginger ale. We ate at the patio table.

After we ate I suggested a game of Frisbee with Cuddles.

"I have to get ready for my date," Regan said.

"It's only two o'clock," I said.

"I have to shave my legs and—" Regan said.

"Shave your legs?" I said. "When did this start?"

"Sister Mary Martin taught me at the hospital like five years ago," Regan said.

"Oh," I said.

"I have to wash my hair, iron my clothes and do my nails and makeup," Regan said.

"Oh," I said.

After Regan went into the house, Oz said, "I'll toss the Frisbee with you."

"What makeup?" I said.

"She wear makeup every day when she go to work," Oz said.

"I guess I never noticed," I said.

"Come on, Wally, the dog want to play," Oz said.

While Wally and Oz tossed the Frisbee around with Cuddles, I went to my office and worked on the reward advertisement for a while.

Around five o'clock I was satisfied it would do the trick. I found Wally and Oz in the living room, watching a movie on television.

I handed Wally the paper. "Read this out loud," I said.

Wally adjusted his glasses and looked at the page. "Header, What's that?" he said.

"The top of the page," I said.

"Reward for information leading to the safe return for missing woman," Wally said. "Ten million dollars is being offered for information that leads to the safe return of Miss Barbara Bouchette who was kidnapped two weeks ago. If you have any information about the kidnappers or the whereabouts of Miss Bouchette, please call this number. All calls will be confidential. The reward is good for one week only."

"That gonna bring the crazies out," Oz said.

"I'm counting on just that," I said.

"When you gonna post it?" Oz said.

"As soon as I pick up a separate cell phone that can handle the volume of calls," I said.

"The phone store at the mall open tomorrow," Oz said.

"Then we'll go shopping tomorrow," I said.

I returned to my office and jotted some notes to myself and waited for six o'clock. When I heard the doorbell ring, I went upstairs to the living room.

Oz opened the door and Tony, a gawky kid with dark hair and eyes and some pimples on his face said, "Hello, sir. I'm Tony, are you Regan's father?"

"Do I look like Regan's father?" Oz said. "I'm almost eighty years old, you—"

"I'm Regan's father," I said. "Come in."

Tony entered and Oz closed the door.

"I'm Tony. I'm here to take Regan to the movies," Tony said.

"It's nice to meet you, Tony," I said. "And this is Wally."

"Regan never mentioned she had a brother," Tony said.

"Oh, no, see, I'm here because of Bubbles," Wally said.

"Because of what?" Tony said.

"See, she used to be a stripper, but we..." Wally said.

"I'm ready," Regan said as she entered the living room.

"You look very nice," Tony said.

"Thank you," Regan said as she handed her car keys to Tony. "You can drive."

"What time will you be home?" I said.

"Movie starts at eight, is over by ten-thirty," Regan said. "We'll go for a snack afterward, say midnight."

"Alright, have a good time," I said.

I watched from the bay window as my daughter and Tony walked to her car. He opened the passenger door for her and then went around and got behind the wheel.

"She be fine," Oz said.

"Yeah," I said.

Standing next to me, Wally said, "They grow up so fast."

"Good Lord," Oz said. "Come on, Wally, I'll play you a video game."

I returned to my office and made some notes to myself and tweaked the ad for a bit. Ten million dollars was a great deal of money, enough to make you rich and change your life. It wasn't the typical cry for help reward that brought out the nut-jobs hoping for some quick, easy money.

Sure, some nut jobs would respond and be quickly dismissed.

But, ten million dollars can also turn a loyal friend, betray a lover and even pit brother against brother.

Around seven o'clock, Jane called on my cell phone.

"How did it go?" she said.

"If you mean Regan's date, he seemed like a nice enough kid," I said.

"Good," Jane said. "How did she look?"

"Like a budding young woman," I said.

"Also good," Jane said. "So I'm tied up doing sheriff stuff until tomorrow. Come by for dinner tomorrow night?"

"Actually, can you come here?" I said. "I'm expecting some phone calls."

"I can. From who?"

"I'll explain tomorrow. What would you like for dinner?"

"Surprise me."

After hanging up with Jane, I went to the living room where oz and Wally were battling for world domination on the television.

"Guys, I'm hungry," I said. "What would you like for dinner?"

"Surprise us," Oz said.

\* \* \*

I was dozing on the sofa when Regan returned home.

"Dad, what are you doing?" she said.

"Waiting up for my daughter," I said.

She sat beside me on the sofa.

"How did it go?" I said.

"Dinner was good, the movie was silly and Tony was a perfect gentleman," Regan said.

"What was the movie?" I said.

"Super heroes save the world nonsense," Regan said.

I stood up. "I'm going to bed now," I said.

"Dad, thanks for waiting up," Regan said.

# Chapter Thirty-two

Wally and I spent the morning placing our quarter page ad in *The New York Times*, *The Daily News* and *New York Post*, the Long Island newspaper, *Newsday* and the White Plains newspaper, *The Caller*.

We scheduled the ad to run from tomorrow for seven days. I told each newspaper I would call back with the contact phone number.

All told, Wally spent more than fifty thousand dollars on the ads for the six newspapers.

"Let's go to the mall for a new phone," I said.

"We take Regan's car," Oz said. "It smell better."

"My car doesn't smell," I said.

"Not much. Smell like a damn ashtray," Oz said. "All them cigarettes ruin your nose."

We took Regan's car to the mall. She drove.

Once inside the mall, Regan took Wally's arm. "Come on, Wally, you need some new shoes," she said.

"What's wrong with my shoes?" Wally said.

"They're older than me and have more scrapes on them than my dad's hands," Regan said. "Come one, let's go."

Oz and I wandered around until we found the phone store. I told a clerk I wanted a phone that could handle a large amount of messages in the in box. Eleven hundred dollars later, I walked out of the store with a phone that did everything except shave my face in the morning.

We left the store and wandered around until we found Regan and Oz in a shoe store. Wally had purchased four new pairs of shoes.

"Oz, do you want anything?" I said.

"Yeah, lunch," Oz said.

*   *   *

Back home, I called the newspapers back and gave them the cell phone contact number.

"Now what?" Wally said.

"We wait," I said. "And while we're waiting I'm going for a workout.

The ads wouldn't break until tomorrow, so after an hour in the backyard, I went for a run on the beach.

The sand was deserted of people, the waves were high, the ocean breeze was refreshing and I let my thoughts go where they may.

The FBI had turned up nothing on hospital and morgue employees. Same for the bonds and kidnapping MOs of a similar nature.

A piece of the puzzle was missing.

A great big piece.

I was convinced Barbara Wilcox didn't have the brain power to mastermind the plan and execute it.

She played her part perfectly, hooking Wally like a hungry bass after the bait. So who was behind the whole thing baiting the hook?

After running three miles on the water's edge, I turned around and ran another three. Then I sat on the sand a few feet from the waves and thought for a while more.

The kidnapping was impeccably planned and executed to

perfection. It took a brilliant mind to work out and time the details down to the last second.

A brilliant mind or…?

I stood up and jogged to my car and drove home.

*   *   *

At my desk I did a computer search of crime and noir novels for plots similar to our case.

After several hours of reading plots of mystery and noir novels, I found what I was looking for.

The novel was titled, The Case of the Missing Fan Dancer. It was written in 1931 by a writer I never head of before. A stripper who preformed with fans meets a wealthy playboy type and they fall in love, only to have her kidnapped and held for ransom. After the ransom is paid, the police find the headless body of a woman in the warehouse where the stripper was supposed to be.

The kidnappers get away with it, but the plot deviates from there. Greed overcomes the two men behind the scheme and the stripper and they wind up killing each other for the money.

I used the hard line phone to call Paul Lawrence in Washington.

"Are you at a computer?" I said.

"Give me a minute," Lawrence said. "Okay, I'm at a computer."

"Search The Case of the Missing Fan Dancer," I said.

"Hold on," Lawrence said. After a minute or so, he said, "It's an old crime novel."

"Read the plot," I said.

After a few seconds, Lawrence said, "You got to be kidding me."

"Our mastermind like to read old crime novels," I said.

"This book has been out of print for ninety years," Lawrence said. "Where would he even find one?"

"I'll let you know when I know," I said.

\*   \*   \*

Jane showed up around seven and found me working at my desk.

"What are you doing?" she said.

"Researching out of print bookstores," I said.

"Whatever for?"

I told her.

"Bekker that brain of yours is always in overdrive," Jane said.

"That's why I need you, to help me turn it off," I said.

Jane looked at me with a funny expression on her face.

"What?" I said.

"You've told me you love me lots of times," she said. "But that's the first time you ever said you needed me."

"Make sure it's not the last," I said.

"Come on, the gang is waiting on us for dinner," Jane said.

\*   \*   \*

After dinner, Jane helped me conduct a search of out of print bookstores.

Manhattan had three. One in the Village, one on the Upper West Side and the third on the Lower East Side.

Queens had one on Queens Boulevard.

Albany had one near the capital.

White Plains didn't have one, but Bronxville did and that was just a few miles away.

There's one in Buffalo, but I doubted he'd travel five hundred miles for a book.

"Tomorrow I make some calls," I said.

"What did you plan to do tonight?" Jane said.

# Chapter Thirty-three

The first day of the ad produced zero calls.

I expected as such. The average person that responds to ads for reward money is looking for a quick hundred and generally is a street snitch junkie.

My ad had to germinate for a while and play on somebody's conscience until temptation overcame guilt.

I spent the morning calling out of print bookstores.

The three in Manhattan didn't have a copy, although two of the three had heard of the book and priced it at three hundred dollars for a first edition, five hundred for an autographed copy. All three stores had calls about the book sometime in the past four to five months.

The store in Queens had never heard of the book until someone called about four or five months ago.

Albany never heard of the book until a caller asked for one. The same for Bronxville.

Buffalo had a copy and sold it four months ago to a collector for three hundred dollars.

"You had the book?" I said. "In your store?"

"Yes sir and like I said it was sold to a collector," the clerk on the phone said.

"Can you give me his name, maybe he'll sell it to me?" I said.

"Please hold," the clerk said.

After holding for several minutes, the clerk returned. "It was sold to a collector named Wallace Sample," he said. "I can call him for you and ask if he would like to sell it to you."

My brain nearly exploded in my head.

"Let me call you back," I said and hung up.

Wally and Regan were playing Frisbee with Cuddles in the backyard. I rushed to Wally and said, "I need to speak with you. Now."

Wally followed me to the office. I sat in my chair and he sat in the chair beside the desk.

"You never mentioned that you were a collector of old books," I said.

"It's a hobby," Wally said. "My psychiatrist suggested it last year when I was having all those problems. I collect old books and baseball cards. I bought a fifty-six Mantle card for thirty thousand."

"You bought a 1931 first edition detective novel titled The Case of the Missing Fan Dancer for three hundred dollars."

"I did? When?

"Four months ago," I said. "Don't you remember?"

"Not really," Wally said. "I have a guy who recommends things to me. He set me up with the Mantle card and maybe a hundred books."

"Where do you keep them?" I said.

"In the den of my condo," Wally said. "It's supposed to be a third bedroom."

I closed my eyes and visualized the disaster that was Wally's condo.

"We're flying to your condo in the morning," I said. "Have your jet fly in tonight and be ready first thing."

"You want me to leave?" Wally said.

"I'm going with you and it's just overnight," I said.

"Alright, I'll call the pilots," Wally said.

"Why don't you relax and go back to Regan and the dog."

"Alright, Mr. Bekker," Wally said.

After Wally left, I called Paul Lawrence.

"I traced a copy of the book from a store in Buffalo, New York to a private collector," I said. "He paid three hundred dollars for it."

"Are you going to tell me who it is?" Lawrence said. "Or are we playing Jeopardy?"

"Wally," I said.

"Our Wally? The fuzzy little butterball?" Lawrence said.

"The one and only," I said. "He collects old books and baseball cards."

"He had it in his possession?" Lawrence said.

"I'm afraid so," I said.

"Where Bouchette and whoever could have picked it up and got the idea for her kidnapping?" Lawrence said.

"I'm afraid so," I said.

"Well Jesus Christ," Lawrence said.

"I'm flying up to Wally's condo in the morning," I said.

"I think I might just join you," Lawrence said.

"Remember where the condo is located?"

"I do."

"We'll meet you there around one tomorrow afternoon," I said.

Before changing into sweats, I checked the cell phone. There wasn't one message.

I got in a solid hour in the backyard and then took a shower and changed and checked the cell phone again. Still no messages.

I packed an overnight bag and then helped Regan with dinner.

"Wally and I are going to new York tomorrow," I said. "Just overnight."

"I'll keep an eye on things," Oz said.

"I know you will," I said.

"Mr. Bekker, I don't remember ever seeing that book," Wally

said. "I didn't even remember ordering it until you reminded me about it."

"Wally, did Barbara stay with you until you got her a place of her own?" I said.

"For a couple of weeks, but she slept in the spare bedroom," Wally said.

"No problem, Wally," I said. "We'll get it figured out."

"Does this have anything to do with the kidnapping?" Wally said.

"Your guess is as good as mine," I said.

*   *   *

After dinner, I took coffee with Oz in the backyard.

"When you gonna tell the fuzzball she played him a sucker?" Oz said.

"I'm not," I said. "Not until it's necessary."

"Keeping truth from him now ain't gonna make it easier for him to swallow the truth later," Oz said.

"I know," I said. "But I can't tell him the entire truth until I know it myself."

"You wait too long and it becomes too late," Oz said.

"I want him to know the truth," I said. "But I don't want to kill him."

"Wait too long and it just might," Oz said.

# Chapter Thirty-four

We had breakfast on the plane. The galley was fully stocked with every kind of microwavable breakfast you could imagine.

I had a breakfast bowl that contained scrambled eggs, sausage and potatoes with two pieces of toast, orange juice and coffee.

Wally had pancakes, waffles, bacon, sausage, toast, juice and ice cream.

"Wally, the book, you said you don't remember it," I said.

"I don't," Wally said. "I have a notebook of the things I buy and keep a record, but I never read the books, I just collect them as part of the hobby. The psychiatrist I needed to see to satisfy the court last year suggested it."

"The man who advises you what to buy, who is he?" I said.

"He's a collector consultant," Wally said. "He works for a collectible company. You sign up for notifications and when he gets wind of things you're interested in, he calls you. He makes a small commission of each sale. As a kid I collected baseball cards and read a lot of mysteries."

"Ever read any of the books you purchased?" I said.

"Who has time to read?" Wally said.

"Right."

Before we landed, I checked the cell phone for messages. The tally was still at zero.

Wally's condo was exactly as I remembered, a disaster of clutter and junk.

The den had a bookcase filled with about one hundred out of print books.

"You bought all these books through that consultant?" I said.

Wally nodded. "Some of them were pretty expensive," he said.

I checked each book in the bookcase. "It's not here," I said.

"Maybe I didn't file it," Wally said.

"Let's check everywhere in every room," I said.

Lawrence arrived when we were checking cabinets in the kitchen.

"The book appears to be missing," I said.

"What a surprise," Lawrence said.

"What is so important about this old book?" Wally said.

Lawrence looked at me. "You didn't tell him?" he said.

"Tell me what?" Wally said.

"The book is about a stripper who fakes her own kidnapping," I said.

Wally stared at me. I could see in his eyes the gears rolling inside his head. His eyes went wide and he said, "Are you saying Barbara had herself kidnapped for the money?"

"I'm afraid so, Wally," I said.

"That can't be true," Wally said. "It can't be."

"I'm afraid it is, Wally," Lawrence said.

Wally flopped onto a chair at the kitchen table. "She used me," he said.

"Wally, there are—" I said.

"To get money," Wally said. "She never cared about me at all."

I looked at Lawrence. "Let's keep looking," I said.

We covered every square inch of the two thousand square foot condo without results. The book was gone.

We returned to the kitchen where Wally was eating a plate of Hot Pockets.

"Wally, your baseball cards, where are they?" I said.

"A floor safe in the closet in the den," Wally said.

We left him to his Hot Pockets and went to the den. The unlocked floor safe was in the closet and empty.

"Well, well," Lawrence said.

On the desk was a ledger book with the baseball cards listed by price and date of purchase. The collection in the safe was worth about one hundred and forty thousand dollars.

"Should we tell him?" Lawrence said.

"Not unless he asks," I said. "You have a car?"

"I do," Lawrence said.

"Let's get Wally and go," I said.

"Where?"

\*　\*　\*

The bouncer at the door recognized us and had us escorted directly to the manager's office. He was behind his desk.

He said, "I saw your ad in the newspaper."

"Is Jackie around?" I said.

"She's on stage," the manager said.

I turned to Lawrence. "Best tell your man we'll be a while," I said.

We left Wally in the car with Lawrence's field agent. Lawrence called his man with the news.

"My guy says Wally's getting antsy," Lawrence said.

"I'll be right back," I said.

I went outside and got into the back seat next to Wally. His eyes were swollen and his face flushed.

"I am what my family says I am, a complete jackass," Wally said.

"That's not true, Wally," I said. "You're naïve and gullible, but you're no jackass. Ask your family how much money you've saved Sample Iced Tea, it's in the tens of millions."

"Maybe so, but they want nothing to do with me," Wally said. "They stuck me in a back office so they don't have to see me or talk to me and they never tell me when there's a board meeting."

"Wally, we all feel the way you're feeling right now," I said. "At some point in our lives we all feel lost and alone but if you give it time it will pass."

"Even you?" Wally said.

"When my wife was murdered my whole life came to a complete stop," I said. "I lost my job, my home and my daughter. I drank too much and hit rock bottom and yet, here I am. Time, Wally. Give it some time."

Wally nodded.

"I need to get back," I said. "I won't be long."

When I returned to the office, Lawrence was alone.

"He went to get the girl," Lawrence said.

A minute later the door opened and Jackie and the manager entered. Lawrence looked at the manager. "Can you wait outside?" Lawrence said.

The manager left and closed the door.

"I saw the ad in the newspaper and if I had anything more I would have called," Jackie said.

"I have just one question," I said. "Did you ever see Barbara reading a book?"

"A book?" Jackie said.

"Yes, a book," I said.

"Maybe once," Jackie said. "Three months ago. She was reading an old book in the lounge."

"Did you see the title?" I said.

"No, but it looked pretty old," Jackie said. "The dust jacket was faded and torn; I remember that much."

"Okay, thanks," I said.

On the way back to the car, Lawrence said, "So she and her partners are looking to take Wally for a ride and finds this novel in Wally's house, reads it and it's off to the races with a fifteen million dollar winning ticket."

"It appears so," I said. "Listen, we have the list of Wally's baseball card collection. See if any have turned up at auction houses or card stores."

"I can do that," Lawrence said.

"Are you staying over?" I said.

"I'm headed back to D.C. as soon as I drop you off," Lawrence said.

"Oh good, I get the big boys room," I said.

# Chapter Thirty-five

W ally and I ordered a vat of Chinese food for dinner and ate at his kitchen table.

"You go back tomorrow," Wally said. "It's time I went back to work anyway."

"No Wally, you're coming home with me," I said.

"Do you think I'm going to hang myself again?" Wally said.

"Remember what I told you what happened to me after my wife was killed?" I said.

"I remember."

"I cut everybody off including Regan," I said. "And I went to a very dark place for ten years. I needed somebody, I needed help and I cut them all off. That's ten years I can't get back. I don't want to see that happen to you."

Wally nodded. "I'll go back with you," he said.

My regular cell phone rang and I picked it up. The incoming call was from the Cupid's Retreat.

"This is Bekker," I said when I answered the call.

"Mr. Bekker, it's the manager of the Cupid's Retreat. After you left, Jackie tole me what you said about Barbara reading a book."

"And?"

"After she left she never came back to clean out her locker," the manager said. "After a month I cleaned it out and put her stuff in storage. I remembered a book and I got it in my office."

154

"What's the title?" I said.

"The Case of the Missing Fan Dancer."

"We'll be there shortly," I said.

I hung up and looked at Wally. "Where's your car?"

"My car?"

"Yes, your car. Where is it?"

"Um, in the basement garage," Wally said. "I think. I haven't see it for a while. I'm not sure I even have one."

"Never mind. Can you call the car service and have them pick us up?" I said.

"As soon as I finish the last egg roll," Wally said.

\* \* \*

"Stay in the car," I said. "I won't be long."

I left the limo and entered the Cupid's Retreat and nodded to the bouncer.

"He's expecting you," he said.

I went to the office and knocked on the door, opened it and stepped inside. The manager was at his desk, the book was on top of it.

"This the book?" he said.

"That's it."

I exchanged the book for a crisp hundred dollar bill.

"I wish I knew more," the manager said. "I could use ten million dollars."

On the way back to the car, I looked at the book. The pages were a bit yellow and dog-eared in several places. I checked and where the pages were dog-eared were fresh bends in the paper.

"Got it," I said to Wally when I sat beside him in the limo.

The driver started north. I handed the book to Wally. He looked it over.

"I don't remember it," he said.

"Could it have come when she was staying with you and opened it herself?" I said.

"Could be."

I took the book back from Wally. "See those little folds on certain pages?" I said.

Wally nodded.

"Some people like to fold the edge to keep their place," I said. "These folds are fresh," I said.

I flipped to the last dog-ear. It was the part in the book where they were planning the kidnapping.

The book arrived. Barbara signed for it, opened it and got an idea from the title and read to the part where they planned the kidnapping. She takes the book to her cohorts and they hatch a plan of their own based on the book.

"The whole thing was just an act to get my money," Wally said. "And I'm the little fool caught in the middle."

"All men are fools for women at some time or another," I said.

"Even you?"

"Even me," I said. "It's how we learn as men. Without making these kinds of mistakes we'd go through life as imbeciles and never learn a thing."

"Maybe I can ask the driver to stop for ice cream on the way home?" Wally said.

"It's after midnight," I said.

"The Friendly's is open all night," Wally said.

\*   \*   \*

Around one in the morning, I sat on the sofa with a bowl of chocolate ice cream and read The Case of the Missing Fan Dancer.

Crime and noir novels were shorter in length back then and

this one tipped the scales at one hundred and seventy pages.

The plot and story rushed by.

The fan dancer met the rich playboy while performing on night on a vaudeville stage one night. The stripper worked her charms on the playboy and the next thing you know he had set her up in a love nest apartment.

Once he was really hooked, the fan dancer was kidnapped by her two partners and held for one hundred thousand dollars ransom. After the ransom was paid, police found the headless body of a woman in a warehouse and the police never found the kidnappers.

The second half of the book was dedicated to the fan dancer and her two male partners. They had gotten away with the perfect crime. They stole the body of the woman from a morgue and escaped the police, but they couldn't escape their own greed and eventually they killed each other leaving the money never to be found.

At 3:00 a.m., I closed the book and went to sleep.

# Chapter Thirty-six

After breakfast, while Wally took a shower, I called Paul Lawrence.

"I have the book," I said.

"The fan dancer book?" Lawrence said. "How?"

"It was delivered when Barbara was staying with Wally before he got her an apartment," I said. "She read it and dog-eared the pages. She stopped reading after they got the money."

"And how do you know she actually read the book?"

"Remember Jackie, she called and told me she remembered her reading it at the club," I said. "Barbara left it behind when she quit and the manager cleared out her locker."

"So they used the book as a diagram for the kidnapping and ransom," Lawrence said. "How does the book end?"

"They get away with it but greed gets the better of them and they kill each other off and the money is never recovered," I said.

"Interesting," Lawrence said.

"I'll call you later, Wally is out of the shower," I said.

"That image will be in my head all day, thank you," Lawrence said.

"Bye," I said.

\* \* \*

"Mr. Bekker, I want to get in shape," Wally said. "Can you help me?"

I was drinking coffee and watching clouds below us fly by. I looked at Wally. "Are you serious?" I said.

"I'm tired of being the butt of every joke and I'm tired of being out of shape," Wally said. "So, yes, I'm serious."

"When was the last time you saw a doctor?" I said.

"What year is it?" Wally said.

"First thing is a physical," I said. "I don't want you dying on me while getting into shape. Agreed?"

"Agreed."

Before we landed, I checked the cell phone for messages. There were none. I wasn't surprised. If anyone called it would have to be the real thing.

* * *

Robert Sample called while I was stretching my legs with a run on the beach before dinner.

"Mr. Bekker, I was wondering if you had any results from the ad you posted in the newspapers," he said.

"Not a peep," I said.

"Well that's off, isn't it?" Robert said. "I would have thought a reward like that would have flooded your phone."

"Just the opposite," I said. "It's designed to bring out only someone who really knows something."

"I can see that," Robert said. "I was wondering how much longer Wally will be staying with you?"

"We had to tell him she was in on it," I said. "He didn't take it too well. I'd like to keep an eye on him until I know for sure he won't hurt himself."

"I understand," Robert said.

I hung up and continued my run. What I didn't tell Robert, or anyone else for that matter was that I hoped Barbara and company saw the ad and realized the FBI and company wasn't going to quit and walk away.

Maybe make them nervous enough to cash those bonds earlier than they planned and expose themselves.

Exposing themselves would leave a trail to follow. Even a small trail of breadcrumbs can lead to a whole loaf."

When I reached home, I showered, changed and sat down to dinner. "Eat good tonight, Wally," I said. "Tomorrow we see a doctor and begin your training."

"What are you talking about?" Regan said. "What doctor?"

"I asked Mr. Bekker to get me shape," Wally said.

"You kidding?" Oz said.

"I really want to do this," Wally said. "For myself."

"Ever hear that sometimes the cure is worse than the disease?" Oz said.

"I'm the disease?" I said.

"If the shoe fit, kick yourself in the ass with it," Oz said. "Wally, Bekker will kill you first before you get in shape."

"I agreed to help, Oz," Regan said. "I'll keep dad in line."

"We start tomorrow," Wally said as he stuffed his mouth with mashed potatoes."

"I best buy a defibrillator on Amazon," Oz said.

\* \* \*

After dinner, Oz and I took coffee in the backyard.

"You were right," I said. "We told him about Barbara and he took it hard."

"That why he came back, so we can keep an eye on him?" Oz said.

"I couldn't leave him alone," I said.

"For a tough guy you all mush on the inside," Oz said.

"Mush is my middle name," I said.

"And what between your ears," Oz said.

"I'll drink to that," I said and Oz and I clinked our coffee cups.

# Chapter Thirty-seven

Before breakfast, I checked the cell phone for messages. There were none.

Breakfast for Wally was oatmeal with a sliced banana and two slices of toast with jelly. Oz, Regan and I showed our moral support for Wally by having the same.

After breakfast, I drove Wally to see our family doctor who gave Wally a complete physical.

"Good Lord, man, your cholesterol is off the charts," the doctor said.

"But is he healthy enough to begin a workout regimen?" I said. "We'll take care of his diet."

"His heart is basically sound, but I would ease into it gradually," the doctor said. "And for God's sake, lay off the fatty foods."

*　*　*

After we returned home, we changed and headed to the backyard, along with Regan.

"The best way to loosen up is with some light skipping rope," I said. "Show him Regan."

Regan took the rope and skipped slowly to the rhythm I had taught her to a while back.

"Now you try it," I said.

Wally was the most uncoordinated individual I had ever met. He tripped, stepped on the rope, dropped the rope and even managed to throw it over the fence, but after much practice he managed to get in ten repetitions without stopping.

"No weights until you strengthen your core a bit," I said.

I had Wally start with push-ups. He managed three before being glued to the ground. He managed five sit-ups and zero pull-ups, but did manage to hang from the bar for ten seconds.

We repeated the process three times.

Then I handed Wally a pair of heavy bag gloves and gave him some basic instruction. He managed three sets of thirty seconds at a time on the bag.

The speed bag which requires skill and coordination and takes years to master we skipped over and headed to the beach in Regan's car.

"We're going to walk one mile at a slow but steady pace," I said.

The mile took thirty minutes to complete. Even a sloth could beat Wally's time, but I was satisfied with the first day's training.

\* \* \*

The afternoon saw no messages on the cell phone. I did a one hour workout in the backyard, grabbed a shower and changed.

Wally was working at his laptop in the living room. He was snacking on a carrot stick. Oz was reading a book in the backyard with Molly on his lap. Regan in the kitchen preparing Wally's dinner.

I went to my office and called Jane.

"Feel like a sleepover?" I said.

"Sure. Let me call my girlfriends and see who's free," Jane said.

"Fair warning, I have Wally on a diet," I said.

"I could lose a few pounds myself," Jane said. "And your correct answer is?"

"Don't change a thing," I said. "I love every inch of you just as you are."

"You learned a few things," Jane said. "See you around six."

After hanging up with Jane, I checked the cell phone and there was one message in the form of a text.

*Please call Jackie at this number*, the message read with the phone number following.

I sat back for a moment and thought. Then I used the cell phone to call Jackie. I got her voice mailbox and left a message.

\* \* \*

I was in the backyard with Oz when Jane arrived. She still wore her sheriff's uniform and carried an overnight bag.

"Hey, Oz," she said as she greeted me with a kiss on the cheek.

"Just put some fresh coffee on, want a cup?" Oz said.

"Sure will," Jane said.

Oz went inside to the kitchen. Jane took the chair next to mine at the patio table.

"So, how is the…" Jane said as the cell phone rang.

It was Jackie calling back.

"This is Bekker," I said.

"Mr. Bekker, it's Jackie from the club," Jackie said.

"Yes, I know."

"I might have something for you," she said.

"I'm all ears," I said.

"Not on the phone, in person."

"Jackie, I—"

"In person," Jackie said. "It has to be in person."

"Where?" I said.

"My apartment in Queens."

"Tomorrow. I'm off tomorrow."

"Give me the address," I said.

I jotted it down on the small notepad I always carry.

"I'll call you from the airport," I said.

When I hung up, Jane was glaring at me with flared nostrils. Oz had returned and set coffee cups on the table and sat beside Jane.

"And whom is Jackie?" Jane said.

"A stripper from the club Barbara worked at," I said.

Oz rolled his eyes. "He we go," he said.

"Did I hear right?" Jane said. "Did you just agree to meet a stripper at her apartment?"

"She has information," I said.

"The train has left the station," Oz said.

"Information, is that what they call it these days?" Jane said.

"She produced the book that—." I said.

"Where?" Jane said.

"Where, what?" I said.

"Did she produce the book?"

"At the strip club."

"So you've been hanging out at strip clubs?"

"The train is off the track," Oz said.

"I haven't been hanging… look, you're a cop. You go where the leads take you, you know that," I said.

"I've never had a lead take me to a male strip club," Jane said.

"I'm not going to a club, I'm going to her apartment," I said.

"And foot goes in mouth," Oz said.

Jane stood up.

"Duck, Bekker, she got a gun," Oz said.

"I'd shoot him in the head but I expect that would do very little damage as it appears to be empty," Jane said.

"Touché," Oz said.

"I'll be in the kitchen with the civilized people," Jane said and marched away.

"Game, set, match," Oz said.

I looked at Oz. "Don't look at me, I ain't meeting no strippers," he said.

*   *   *

From my desk, I called Lawrence on the hard line phone.

"I'm going to New York tomorrow to see Jackie," I said.

"The stripper?"

"She called and said she has something she wants me to see," I said.

"And that is?"

"She wouldn't tell me," I said. "I have to go to her apartment."

After a short pause, Lawrence said, "You know, when I was a kid there was this TV show. The kid with the robot and whenever the kid got into trouble, the robot would say 'warning, warning, danger, Wil Robinson.'"

"Paul, do you know how long I've been doing this?" I said.

"Long enough to know better than to meet a stripper at her apartment," Lawrence said. "It's like fighting a battle in a basement. Nobody wins."

"Look, she got us the book, I'd like to see what else she has," I said. "Let me rephrase that. I'd like to—"

"I know what you meant," Lawrence said. "I could have a man meet you and pick you up at the airport."

"Not necessary," I said. "And I'll call you the minute I find out what it is."

After I hung up, Jane came down to the basement. "Your daughter is making skinless baked chicken, broccoli, beets and peas," she said.

"It's part of Wally's diet plan," I said.

"Can we go out for a burger later?" Jane said.

"I thought you were mad at me," I said.

"Whatever gave you that idea?" Jane said.

"You… in the backyard… you practically tore my head off," I said.

"Oh that," Jane said. "I got over that. Come on, dinner is on the table."

*   *   *

Around ten o'clock, we snuck away and I drove to a burger joint near the mall. We went in and ordered burgers with fries and glasses of ginger ale.

"What time are you leaving?" Jane said.

"Best I could do is a ten am out and a midnight home," I said.

"I'll stay over," Jane said.

"Want dessert?" I said.

"When we get back, you can give me all the dessert you want to," Jane said.

# Chapter Thirty-eight

The plane landed at Kennedy Airport a few minutes before ten am and taxied to out gate right on time.

I rented a car, entered the address Jackie gave into the GPS and called her from my cell phone before I left the airport.

"Mr. Bekker?" Jackie said.

"I'm at Kennedy," I said. "I should be at your apartment in thirty minutes or so."

"Ring the buzzer for apartment 6B," Jackie said.

"See you in a while," I said.

I left the airport and took the Long Island Expressway to Queens Boulevard and drove about seven miles to the neighborhood known as Key Gardens.

Jackie's apartment was located in a twenty-story condo on 67street one block off Queens Boulevard.

I parked on the street, entered the outer lobby and rang the bell for apartment 6B. A buzzer sounded and I opened the inner lobby door. There were four elevators and I took one of them to the 6th floor.

Jackie was waiting in the hallway beside her open door.

"I made a fresh pot of coffee," she said.

I entered the apartment and she closed the door. She was wearing jeans with a T-shirt and was barefoot. Her toenails were painted a deep red.

"Come have a cup and I'll tell you why I called," Jackie said.

We went to the kitchen where Jackie filled two cups with coffee and then we took chairs at the table.

"Nice apartment," I said.

"It isn't mine," Jackie said. "It's a sublet."

I tried the coffee. It was pretty good. "So why did I come all this way?" I said.

"Remember when you asked me about Barbara's boyfriends and fans?" Jackie said.

"I remember," I said.

"I don't know why I didn't think of this right away," Jackie said. "I'm not too bright I guess or I wouldn't be stripping for a living. Anyway, about a year ago the manager got the idea of filming the headliners shows and selling them as DVDs. Barbara sold about fifty a week at fifteen a pop. Anything for money, right?"

"What did you find?" I said.

"I have ten of her DVDs and I watched all of them," Jackie said. "They manager has three cameras set up and in all of them you can see the same guy front and center."

"Let's take a look," I said.

"Living room," Jackie said.

We went to the living room and sat on the sofa.

"This has to be worth something, right?" Jackie said. "Maybe not ten million but something."

"Show me what you got," I said.

Jackie hit a button on a remove and the television played Barbara's balloon dance.

"I watched all ten and just watch," Jackie said. "There, that guy," she said and hit the pause button.

I stood up, walked to the television and looked at the face of Chuck Ludin.

"You know the guy, don't you?" Jackie said.

"I want to see all ten," I said.

We watched one hundred and fifty minutes of Barbara's bubble dance and Ludin was in a front row seat at each performance.

"When was the last DVD recorded?" I said.

"Right before she quit I think. I wasn't paying much attention at the time."

"I'm taking all ten," I said.

"I didn't risk my job for free," Jackie said.

"Don't worry, you'll be compensated," I said. "I'll see to that."

"Well, now that we got that out of the way, I'm off today and have nothing to do," Jackie said. "Maybe you'd like to stick around and we could get to know each other."

"Jackie, the belt I'm wearing is older than you," I said.

"Age is just a number," Jackie said. "Besides, you don't look so old to me."

"I'll have a check sent to you when I get home," I said.

"I get pretty lonely here by myself," Jackie said. "I don't get to meet many real men in my line of work. I could really use the company."

"Tell you what," I said. "Go change and I'll take you to lunch. That's the best I can do."

Jackie nodded. "Give me five minutes," she said.

\* \* \*

There was a nice, family-style diner in Forest Hills on Queens Boulevard. We settled into a booth by a window and ordered coffee.

"You're probably wondering how I got into stripping," Jackie said.

"I wasn't but if you feel like telling me I'll listen," I said.

Jackie sipped coffee and then smiled weakly. "I'm from Ohio," she said. "I came to New York when I was eighteen to study dance at Julliard. That was eight years ago."

"What happened?" I said.

"What usually happens," Jackie said. "I blew out a knee and bye-bye dance career. I had three room mates in an apartment on West 63rd and two of them were strippers, although they are called exotic dancers these days. I could go home or I could stay. I could stave or I could make money. I chose to make money. I give myself three more years before I have enough saved to go back to Ohio and open my own dance studio."

The waitress came by and we ordered omelets with bacon and potatoes, toast and juice.

"What about you, how did you become a private detective?" Jackie said.

"I was a police detective assigned to organized crime," I said. "I got too close. They came for me and murdered my wife instead. I retired and now I do this."

"Jeez, life is fucked sometimes, isn't it?" Jackie said.

"You take the good with the bad and hope in the end there is more good," I said.

"Yeah. The truth is I was hoping to make some extra money by bringing you those DVDs and maybe chop some time off those three years," Jackie said.

"I'll make sure of that when I get home," I said. "Who knows, you might wind up with all of it."

"A tiny slice of the pie would be nice," Jackie said.

"I'll call you when I get home," I said.

"Do you have someone now?" Jackie said.

"I do."

"Lucky woman."

"Just the opposite," I said.

"I guess you have to go now," Jackie said.

"Maybe we'll have a slice of apple pie first," I said.

\*   \*   \*

I called Paul Lawrence from the airport.

"I have something you should see," I said.

"From the stripper?" Lawrence said.

"Yes. I'll bring it to you so you can burn copies," I said.

"Are you going to tell me what it is?" Lawrence said.

"Nope. I hate to ruin a good surprise," I said. "Expect me day after tomorrow."

\*   \*   \*

I unlocked the front door as quietly as possible and entered, closed the door and locked it again.

Nightlights gave off enough light for me to make it safely to the basement where I set my overnight bag on the floor beside the day bed.

I stripped down to T-shirt and shorts and got into bed beside Jane's warm body. I wasn't expecting her to be in the day bed and she woke up.

"This better be Bekker and not Wally," she said.

"I didn't mean to wake you," I said. "Go back to sleep."

"I don't want to sleep," Jane said. "I want to fool around."

"Work, work, work," I said as Jane got on top of me.

# Chapter Thirty-nine

Before breakfast, I showed Jane one of the DVDs on the set in the basement.

"So that's Bubbles, huh," she said.

I paused the picture. "See that guy in the audience?" I said/

"The one with drool on his chin?" Jane said.

"That guy works in the Sample Iced Tea warehouse and claims to have made the call to hire her for the bachelor party," I said. "He claims he never saw her before the night of the party."

"He claims a lot," Jane said.

"He does."

"Let me guess, he's on the other nine DVDs," Jane said.

"Good guess," I said.

"Now what?"

"I see Paul in D.C.," I said.

"He could just be guilty of being a man obsessed with fake tits," Jane said.

"He could."

"But you don't think so."

"I don't."

"I have to go to work," Jane said. "I'll see you later."

\*     \*     \*

After Wally had a breakfast of two poached eggs with toast and jam, orange juice and coffee, we went to the backyard for his workout.

Regan didn't have to be at work until noon and joined us. We took it easy on Wally and he managed to get through the workout without collapsing.

"Okay, let's head to the beach for our walk," I said.

Regan left for work. I took my car to the beach and Oz and Cuddles joined us.

I upped the distance to a mile and a quarter and increased the pace just a bit. Oz and Cuddles had no problem keeping up even if Wally struggled a bit.

After we completed the mile and a quarter, we sat on the sand for a while and watched the waves glisten in the sun.

Oz put his arm around Wally. "You know, boy, we all got a lot to live for," he said.

\* \* \*

Late in the afternoon, I watched all ten DVDs again. I noted the time on each one where Ludin was visible in the audience.

On the third DVD, I saw Barbara wink in his direction.

On the fifth DVD, it appeared she blew him a kiss.

On the ninth DVD, she winked and blew him a kiss.

All were subtle and if you weren't examining them carefully it went by in a flash.

Satisfied, I packed them away in my overnight bag.

\* \* \*

I left the house at 6am to catch my eight o'clock flight to Washington. Traffic was light and I arrived in plenty of time to grab an overpriced breakfast sandwich at the airport.

By noon, I was in a cab headed to the FBI Headquarters building in Washington.

A guard called up to Lawrence and he met me in the lobby with a visitor's pass.

"Do you want lunch first or show and tell?" Lawrence said.

"Lunch," I said. "I've been up since five."

"Come on, the cafeteria serves a decent burger," Lawrence said.

I followed Lawrence, suitcase in hand to the cafeteria. It was quite busy and we were lucky to find a table for two.

I left my suitcase on my chair and we went through the cafeteria-style serving line. We both selected bacon burgers with fries. I went with ginger ale and Lawrence grabbed a Coke.

"So you're really not going to tell me until we in the office," Lawrence said.

I fished out the book and handed it to Lawrence. "Note the dog eared pages end after the kidnapping," I said.

Lawrence rifled through the worn, yellowing pages. "They were probably figuring their play when this shows up in the mail and gives them a perfect blueprint," he said.

"My guess is they were going to film Wally in compromising positions and extort money from him and the book changed their minds," I said.

We finished lunch and took containers to Lawrence's office.

"We need a DVD player," I said.

"Conference room," Lawrence said.

One flight up was a large conference room that wasn't in use. I opened my suitcase and removed the ten DVDs.

"The manager of the Cupid's Retreat came up with the idea of filming the headliner's shows and selling them as DVDs," I said. "There are ten of Barbara's shows."

I took out my notebook and noted the time where to pause the disc. Then I hit play.

"Good quality," Lawrence said. "Almost professional."

I hit the pause button at the three minute mark and pointed to Ludin.

"Recognize this guy?" I said.

"The guy from the warehouse," Lawrence said.

"Charles Ludin, the man who claimed he called Cupid's Retreat at random," I said.

"He's on every DVD?"

"She even blows him kisses and winks," I said.

"Son of a bitch," Lawrence said.

"Can your guys burn off copies and print photos of every frame Ludin is in?" I said.

"They'll love this one," Lawrence said.

"Ludin isn't the brains," I said. "Neither is Barbara. She may have stumbled across the book and read it, but neither has the criminal IQ or experience to organize and pull it off."

"The third party with access to the hospital morgue?" Lawrence said.

"Background check Ludin from birth," I said. "His family and friends, everybody who might know the man."

"That could take some time."

"Time we got," I said. "Evidence we don't."

"We sure don't," Lawrence said. "No judge in his right mind would issue an arrest warrant based upon a face in a strip joint video."

"Maybe so, but I don't need a warrant to stir the pot a bit," I said.

"You mean confront him?" Lawrence said.

"Talk to him," I said.

"I've seen how you talk, Jack," Lawrence said. "I'd hate to be on the other end of that conversation."

"Can you have those photos done by morning?" I said. "I'm staying over."

"First tell me what you're planning," Lawrence said.

"Nothing yet," I said. "But if I decide to have a talk with him I'd like to be able to rattle his nerves when he denies knowing her."

"I suppose it wouldn't do any good to tell you to leave this to us, would it?" Lawrence said.

"I've been hired by Wally and represent Frank Kagan's firm," I said. "I have an obligation to my clients."

"What does Kagan have to do with this?" Lawrence said.

"Not a thing, but it's legal," I said.

"I could pull rank."

"You could but I'm not bound to listen," I said. "Besides, it would be years before you're men would crack the file open again. Let's meet for breakfast. I'm going to my hotel room and take a nap."

"I didn't think you were the napping kind," Lawrence said.

"Sure I am," I said. "I once napped for ten years."

# Chapter Forty

I met Lawrence for breakfast at the dining room in the lobby of my hotel. He had a large manila envelope under his right arm and set it on the table.

"The original DVDs and eight-by-eleven photos of Ludin," Lawrence said as he took a chair.

A waitress came by and I ordered an omelet with bacon and potatoes, toast, juice and coffee.

"Make that two," Lawrence said.

"Last night I was thinking," I said.

The waitress came back with two cups of coffee.

"And?" Lawrence said.

"Let's talk to a federal judge," I said.

"I told you last night, based on what we have we'd be laughed out of chambers," Lawrence said.

"I know," I said. "But it would give us the opportunity to find out what it would take to get a warrant instead of guessing."

Lawrence looked at me and nodded. "We'll see a judge right after breakfast," he said.

\*   \*   \*

Warren Springfield was appointed a federal judge fifteen years ago and had the reputation as a no nonsense but fair minded judge.

He was tall, thin and had silver hair and liquid blue eyes.

He knew Lawrence well and agreed to see us at ten that morning.

Lawrence spoke first and then turned it over to me. I asked for and was granted permission to show a DVD and then presented the photographs.

He made notes but didn't interrupt and waited until I had finished talking.

"Mr. Bekker, is it?" he said.

"Yes, your honor," I said.

"I hold with the theory that when a man lies it is for a reason," Springfield said. "However, as far as I can determine I can not link the kidnapping to Mr. Ludin based upon the face that he enjoyed going to a strip club. Therefor I am declining your request for a warrant."

"We understand that, your honor," I said. "What would it take to get a warrant if we should reapply?"

"Evidence that links him directly to the crime," Springfield said. "Of which you have none at the moment I'm afraid."

\* \* \*

I sat on a bench with Lawrence in the National Mall, which is a landscaped park and looked at the Washington Monument in the distance.

"Call me when your guys have finished background info on Ludin," I said.

"I will but even if we uncover that his first cousin is a hospital morgue attendant, it doesn't link him to the kidnapping," Lawrence said. "It's circumstantial at best and that won't satisfy Springfield or any other judge."

"I know," I said.

"I want this guy as much as you, but I don't want him to walk on a technicality," Lawrence said.

"I have to catch my plane," I said. "Call me later when you have the background info."

* * *

The flight home was uneventful and I read a newspaper and then thought about evidence that would satisfy Judge Springfield.

There had to be a direct connection from Ludin to the kidnapping or a warrant wouldn't be granted.

When I opened the front door to my house, no one came to greet me. I found Oz and Wally in the backyard. Wally was doing push-ups and Oz was supervising from a chair.

In the background, Molly and Cuddles wrestled with each other.

Wally got his feet, gasped and looked at me. "I did seven and I've lost three pounds," he said.

"What you stopping for, you know what come next," Oz said.

Wally nodded and put on the bag gloves.

I sat beside Oz.

"Boy is serious about this exercise crap," Oz said.

"Keeps his mind occupied and it's good for him," I said. "Regan at her job?"

Oz nodded. "And Jane stopping by around seven."

"I think I'll change and join Wally," I said.

"Good. I can go read my book now," Oz said.

I changed and got in a full workout. Wally finished up and sat at the patio table and watched until I was done.

"Walk on the beach?" he said.

"Walk on the beach," I said.

We took my car to the beach where I parked in the municipal lot. We walked onto the sand and toward the water. Several hundred yards in we passed a team of land surveyors.

"For the condo's they're going to build," I said.

After three quarters of a mile, we turned around and headed back. The last hundred yards I opened it up to a quick jog and Wally gasped to keep the pace but he managed to finish on his feet.

We sat on the sand for a few minutes and watched the waves.

"Mr. Bekker, I realize I'm being a pest and a nuisance and I've put everybody out," Wally said. "But I'm grateful to you and Oz and Regan. I owe you my life."

"Wally, everybody needs help at sometime in their life. I'm just glad we were able to be there for you," I said. "Now let's get back and take a shower and get ready for dinner."

\* \* \*

When I was a police detective and I was stumped on a case, I would go back to the beginning and look at everything, every detail no matter how small and searched for the detail I had missed.

There is always something, some little something that skipped past your eye. Sometimes the work is repetitious and boring but necessary. Sometimes all it takes is a tiny crack in the dam for the waters to flood. Other times you go hungry.

Going hungry means the crime goes unsolved. Eighty percent of all murders go unsolved. The same for kidnappings.

They're still trying to solve the Lindbergh baby case from ninety years ago.

I was watching the DVDs again when Jane arrived.

"Didn't I leave you like this yesterday morning?" she said.

She kissed me and sat on my lap. "I got to hand it to her, she knows her way around a balloon," she said.

"We struck out with a federal judge," I said. "He wants actual evidence that links Ludin to the crime before issuing a warrant."

"Party pooper," Jane said. "Come on, your daughter slaved over a hot stove to make dinner, the least you can do is eat it."

The table was set with salad bowls. I'm not much for salad, but to keep Wally's spirits up, I ate a bowl. Then came skinless, baked chicken, carrots, peas and corn. Dessert was one chocolate chip cookie.

Dessert of coffee and cookie was served at the backyard patio table. I broke my cookie in two and ate the first half and was about to eat the other half when something clicked in my mind and I stood up and went to my office in the basement.

"Jack, what is it?" Jane said.

"Be right back," I said.

I went to my desk and loaded the first DVD into the player and watched it from the beginning.

Then I saw it, the detail I had skipped over previously. Standing next to Ludin was large man of around forty. I estimated him at around six-five and two fifty or more in weight. He was chatting with Ludin and having a fine time.

"Jack, what's wrong?" Jane said as she entered the office.

I hit reverse and showed Jane the man next to Ludin. "Him," I said.

"What about him?" Jane said.

I played the second and third DVD and the same guy was with Ludin on both.

"Did you check the others?" Jane said.

"Not yet."

We watched the remaining seven DVD and the same guy was at Ludin's side in each one.

"The third guy in the kidnapping plot?" Jane said.

"Could be," I said.

"Let's celebrate by you taking me for some ice cream," Jane said.

# Chapter Forty-one

There's a place not far from the house, a good, old fashioned ice cream stand that serves homemade ice cream and stays open until ten.

Jane and I got bowls of chocolate ice cream and sat at a picnic table.

"I need to call Paul," I said.

"It's nine-thirty," Jane said.

"He'll be up," I said.

"It can wait until morning," Jane said. "I'm sure you'll want to document and write a report before you call him. Besides, the ice cream puts me in the mood."

"Ice cream does?" I said.

"So does chocolate," Jane said. "Remember that come Valentine's Day."

We finished our ice cream and I drove us back to the house. We entered the basement office through the door off the hallway.

I sat in my chair at the desk.

"Oh no you don't," Jane said and turned off the light, leaving just the night light on. "Come undress me like you mean it."

I stood up.

"Start with my holster," Jane said. "The gun is heavy."

*   *   *

Jane and I drank coffee as we watched all ten DVDs again in the morning.

We made some notes. I was about to call Lawrence when I checked the time.

"Shouldn't you be at work by now?" I said.

"I thought you'd never notice," Jane said. "I took the day off. Sheriff's prerogative."

"Did we have breakfast?" I said.

"No, Jack, we didn't," Jane said.

"We'll call him after we have breakfast," I said.

\*   \*   \*

"What's this?" Jane said.

"Oatmeal," Regan said.

Jane looked at me.

"With sliced bananas and some cinnamon it's really good," Wally said.

"And with two slices of toast with jelly it's really filling," Wally said.

Jane looked at Wally.

"I lost four pounds," Wally said.

"Oh dear God," Jane said.

\*   \*   \*

"Paul, I have you on speaker phone," I said. "Jane is with me."

"Hi, Jane," Lawrence said.

"Hello, Paul, it's been a while," Jane said.

"So what do I owe the honor?" Lawrence said.

"The forest for the tree, Paul." I said.

"What am I, a lumberjack now?" Lawrence said.

184

"Put the first DVD in the player and turn it on," I said. "I'll wait."

"Hold," Lawrence said.

He was gone about a minute and then said, "Now what?"

"A minute and three seconds pause it," I said.

After a few seconds, Lawrence said, "Paused."

"See that thick lump on Ludin's right?" I said.

"I see him."

"He's with Ludin on every DVD," I said.

"Son of a bitch if I missed him every time," Lawrence said.

"Forest for the trees," I said.

"I don't think it's good enough for face recognition," Lawrence said.

"Probably not, but maybe Jackie might recognize him," I said.

"Jackie again," Jane said.

"And the Sample family," I said.

"When are you going?"

"Tomorrow."

"I'm tied up."

"No problem, Jane will go with me," I said.

"Jane will?" Jane said.

"Call me with whatever you find," Lawrence said.

"Don't I always."

I hung up and Jane said, "Jane will go with you where?"

"New York. Specifically White Plains," I said.

"Just like that, huh?"

"You haven't taken a vacation in ten years," I said. "An overnight trip isn't going to kill you. And besides, it's good training for when you retire and we become partners."

"I'll need to go home and pack a bag," Jane said.

"While you do that, I'm going to put Wally through his paces," I said.

*   *   *

The highlights of Wally's workout was that he managed eight push-ups, ten sit-ups and half a pull-up before we headed to the beach.

I upped our walk to a mile and three quarters and forced Wally to sprint the last hundred yards.

At the end, he flopped on his back and gasped for air for a solid five minutes. Then we sat for a bit and watched the waves.

"I think it's more fun getting out of shape than getting into shape," Wally said.

"I can't argue with that," I said.

*   *   *

Back home, I did my regular workout and afterward reserved two tickets to New York and followed that up with a call to Jackie.

"I was just leaving for work," she said.

"There's another man I want you to take a look at," I said. "Tomorrow."

"Okay," Jackie said. "What time?"

"Are you working tomorrow?"

"Three to one."

"I'll stop by the club."

"Okay," Jackie said.

After Jackie, I tried Robert Sample's office.

"Mr. Bekker, I was wondering when I'd hear from you," Robert said.

"I'm flying up to see you tomorrow," I said. "Can you make it around two."

"I can. Do you need everybody?"

"It wouldn't hurt."

"What shall I tell them the meeting is about?" Robert said.

"Show and tell," I said.

Robert chuckled. "See you at two," he said.

After a shower, Jane returned with a suitcase.

"Just in time," I said.

"For what?" Jane said.

"Yeah, for what?" Oz said as he entered the living room.

"As soon as Regan get home from her job, I'm taking all of us to dinner," I said.

"Oh dear God, thank you baby Jesus, I can't eat one more beet." Oz said.

# Chapter Forty-two

We skipped the cream of wheat sprinkled with bananas and blueberries and ate a late breakfast at the airport.

Jane wore designer jeans, a white blouse with a blue sports jacket. The two inch heels bumped her up to five foot eleven or so.

We had breakfast at terminal restaurant. Egg sandwiches with bacon and potato patties and coffee.

"Nothing against oatmeal, but," Jane said as she chomped on a potato patty.

"Did you pack your off duty?" I said.

"In my suitcase," Jane said. "I cleared it at check-in. My permit is reciprocal."

"So is mine, but I left it home," I said.

"Don't worry, I'll protect you," Jane said.

"They're calling our flight," I said.

We walked to our gate.

"By the way, where are we staying?"

"Marriott in White Plains," I said.

"Good. It's been a while since I soaked in a hot tub."

\*   \*   \*

I rented a car at the private airfield and drove to the Sample headquarters building in the heart of White Plains.

"It hasn't changed much," Jane said.

"It's only been a year since you were last here," I said.

The lobby guard called up to Robert and then we took the elevator. Robert, Susan, Steven, Amy and Barbara were in the conference room.

"Sheriff Jane Morgan, is that correct?" Robert said.

"It is," Jane said.

"Do you remember Steven, Amy, Susan and Barbara?" Robert said.

"I do," Jane said.

"Can we get on with this?" Barbara said. "We all have work to do."

"Robert, can you turn on the television and DVD player, please?" I said.

"Sure," Robert said. "Help yourself to coffee."

I poured coffee two cups of coffee while Robert went to the television and DVD player. I removed the first disc from my overnight bag and gave it to him.

"You can fast forward to a minute and three seconds and freeze it," I said.

Robert hit the play button.

"Oh, lovely. Wally's hoe in action," Barbara said.

"Stop at a minute three," I said.

Robert fast forwarded the DVD and hit pause at a minute three.

"Right there, see him?" I said.

"Who is that?" Robert said.

"Charles Ludin," I said. "He works in your warehouse. He claims he never met Barbara Bouchette before the bachelor party. We have him on ten different DVDs at her private shows."

"Do you think he's connected to the kidnapping?" Robert said.

"That we don't know. Yet. See the big guy with him, have you ever seen him before?" I said.

"I can't say as I have," Robert said.

"Mind if we ask Ed Post?" I said.

"Not at all," Robert said.

"Thanks," I said. "We'll get back to you."

"I can hardly wait," Barbara said.

Jane looked at her with flared nostrils. I said nothing and looked at my watch. "Honey, if you're going to act the part of tough bitch, can you back it up?" Jane said.

Barbara looked at Jane but kept silent.

"We'll get back to you later," I said.

In the elevator, I said, "Was that necessary?"

"Yes, it was very necessary," Jane said.

\* \* \*

Jane drew her usual reaction as we walked through the warehouse to Ed Post's office, which was open mouths and stares.

"Mr. Bekker, I'm surprised to see you again," Post said.

"Hello, Ed, this is my associate Jane Morgan," I said.

Post stood to shake Jane's hand and they were eye level to each other.

I closed the office door and said, "This is a confidential visit that can't leave your office," I said.

"What's this about?" Post said.

"We need a television and DVD player," I said.

"The meeting room," Post said.

We followed Post to the locked meeting room. He unlocked the door with a key and turned on the lights. A television with a DVD player was on a cabinet opposite the conference table.

There was a large window that overlooked the floor. "Lock the door and close the drapes," I said.

While Post did that, I turned on the television and inserted disc one.

"That's the stripper," Post said.

"It is," I said. "And who is this?"

I hit the pause button.

Post looked closely at the television. "Charles Ludin," he said.

"I have ten of these and he's on every one of them," I said. "And he denied knowing her."

Post looked at me.

"See the big man next to him? He's with Ludin on all ten," I said. "Do you recognize him?"

Post stared at the television. "Why, that's Bo Dorn. I'm sure of it."

I looked at Jane, then at Post. "Have a file on him?" I said.

*     *     *

Jane wore a neon blue bikini into the hot tub beside the pool. Some young men were in the pool and they stared at Jane as she walked across the tiles and slinked into the hot tub next to me.

I had my regular cell phone and the employee file for Bo Dorn. I was on hold, waiting for Paul Lawrence to come on the line.

"What do we do next?" Jane said.

"Get some dinner and then go see Jackie," I said.

"I thought you wanted to talk to this Ludin?" Jane said.

"I think we'll wait on that until Paul gets back to us," I said. "We'll go to the strip club and get back to Ludin later."

"Every girl's dream date, to go to a strip club and talk to a stripper," Jane said.

"I think they're called exotic dancers these days," I said.

"You can call my foot a Porsche it's still my foot," Jane said.

Lawrence came on the line. "Jack, you got something for me?" he said.

"Bo Dorn," I said. "Real name is Beauregard Wilton Dorn."

"Jesus," Lawrence said.

"From Arkansas. DOB puts him at thirty-nine. He worked on the line with Ludin for about three months after he got out of prison according to his work file at Sample. One day he up and quit. He's the guy with Ludin on the DVDs."

"Can you fax his file to me and I'll run his record," Lawrence said.

"As soon as we get out of the hot tub," I said.

"Hot tub?" Lawrence said.

"It comes with the room," I said.

"Jane in the hot tub with you?" Lawrence said.

"Yes and keep your thoughts to yourself," I said.

"I'll call you later," Lawrence said.

"I'm hungry," Jane said.

"Me too," I said.

*   *   *

"This place gives me the creeps," Jane said as we entered the Cupid's Retreat.

The bouncer at the door nodded to me. "He's in his office," he said.

I took Jane's arm and led her past the stage and she paused. "How does she do that?" she said. "I'd pull a hamstring. I mean, how…?"

"Ask her later," I said.

I knocked on the manager's door.

"It's open," he said.

I opened the door and we entered. Behind his desk, the manager looked at Jane.

"Close your mouth, buster," Jane said. "I'm not here for an audition."

"My partner Jane Morgan," I said. "We want you to look at other of your patrons. Jackie, too."

"Was that book helpful?" the manager said.

"We need to use your television and DVD player," I said.

"Be my guest," the manager said.

I set it up and played the first disc and paused it at the minute three mark.

"Him. The big guy there," I said and pointed my finger.

"Looks familiar," the manager said. "I couldn't tell you who he is."

"Jackie available?" I said.

"I'll call her," the manager said.

A few minutes later, Jackie entered the office. Jackie and Jane sized each other up before Jackie said, "What can I do for you, Mr. Bekker?"

Jane rolled her eyes.

"Take a look at the DVD again and tell me you recognize the big man with the man you identified," I said.

"Yeah, I've seen him. But not recently," Jackie said. "Is he involved?"

"We don't know who is involved at this point," I said.

Jackie looked at Jane. "Is she your lucky woman?" she said.

Jane's eyes narrowed and I cut her off by saying, "Thanks for the help. We'll be in touch."

"Lucky woman my ass," Jane said as we walked back to the car.

"Jane, she didn't mean anything by—" I said.

"Oh shut up and get in the car," Jane said.

\* \* \*

Jane sprawled out on the king size bed in our room.

"Oh Mr. Bekker, is there anything else I can do for you?" she said.

"As I can barely walk, I think you've done enough," I said.

"Turn out the light, I'm tired," Jane said.

"Thank God," I said.

"Light."

I clicked off the lamp.

"Do you know what the difference between Jackie and me is?" Jane said.

"You're taller," I said.

"Mine are real, Jack," Jane said. "You don't go out for beef jerky when you have steak at home."

"Which one of us is the steak?" I said.

"Shut up, hold me and go to sleep," Jane said.

# Chapter Forty-three

After breakfast, while Jane got her nails done in the hotel spa, I grabbed a workout in the hotel gym.

We met afterward at the pool and sat in the hot tub to wait for Lawrence to call.

"This is a really tough job you have," Jane said. "I'm going to like being your partner."

"So, you're officially handing in your papers?" I said.

Jane held out her hands. "How do you like my nails?" she said.

They were neon blue, matching her bikini. "Very nice," I said.

"See anything missing?" Jane said.

"All ten are accounted for," I said.

"Look closer. The ring finger of my left hand. Something is missing," Jane said. "I wonder what it is?"

"Oh," I said.

"Yeah, oh," Jane said. "I swear to God, Bekker, how did you ever get Carol to marry you, as dumb as you are?"

"She asked me," I said.

"Don't hold your breath waiting for me to ask you. You'll die alone and blue in the face," Jane said. "You get me a ring and I'll turn in my papers."

"I'll go shopping as soon as I'm done with this case," I said.

"And don't cheap out like my first husband did, that's why he's an *ex*," Jane said. "I won't have two ex's in my life. I'd just shoot

195

you and bury you in the backyard."

Before I could respond, Lawrence called on my cell phone.

"Good morning, Paul," I said.

"Still in White Plains?" Lawrence said.

"Yes. Specifically, in the hot tub," I said.

"Jane with you?"

"Don't be a lecherous old man," I said.

"This guy Dorn," Lawrence said.

"I'm putting you on speaker," I said.

"Hello, Jane," Lawrence said. "How's the water?"

"I can feel you leering from here, Paul," Jane said.

"About Dorn?" I said.

"Right," Lawrence said. "First arrest for stealing a car in Little Rock at age sixteen," he continued. "In and out of prison a dozen times for you-name-it. He wound up in New York working as a collector for a big time loan shark in Manhattan. Did eighteen months at Riker's for assault after nearly killing a man who owed money to the loan shark. He was released on parole and got a job at Sample on a work release program. After a few months, he vanished."

"About the time he hooked up with Ludin," I said.

"Dorn is listed as six-five, two-seventy-five," Lawrence said. "And he likes to throw his weight around."

"I think we'll have another talk with Ludin," I said.

"We should take over now, Jack," Lawrence said. "I can fly in tonight and we can talk to Ludin together."

"What's Ludin's and Wilcox's records look like?" I said.

"Ludin is clean. Wilcox has a few shoplifting changes from ten years ago in Pittsburgh," Lawrence said.

"So Dorn has to be the catalyst in the trio," I said.

"I'll see you for dinner tonight," Lawrence said. "Sit in the hot tub until I get there."

I hung up and set the phone on the tiled floor.

"It doesn't seem fair that you do all the work and the FBI swoops in like a vulture at the last minute," Jane said.

"We have all afternoon to kill, any suggestions?" I said.

"We could go back to the room and you can help me out of this wet bikini," Jane said. "Or we could watch TV? Pick."

"I don't know, what's on?" I said.

\* \* \*

"Jack, how much do you weigh?" Jane said.

"Two-forty. Why? Did I hurt you?" I said.

"No, you're always gentle with me," Jane said. "But if you're two-forty, this Dorn must be a monster."

"Before we label him anything, we don't know that he or Ludin are responsible for the kidnapping, or any of it," I said.

"But you think so?" Jane said.

"Yeah, I think so," I said. "But it doesn't matter what I think. It only matters what we can prove, and so far, all we can prove is that Ludin and Dorn like strip clubs, and Wilcox read an old book."

"Let's shower and get dressed," Jane said. "Paul should be here soon."

\* \* \*

We waited in the hotel bar. Jane had a glass of wine, while I had a ginger ale.

Around 7:30, Lawrence walked in. He greeted Jane with a kiss on the cheek.

We went to the restaurant and found a table.

"Judging by tomorrow's conversation with Ludin, it might be time to make it official and bring him in," Lawrence said.

"And tell a judge what?" I said. "He's just going to be cut loose by even a junior PD lawyer."

"Out of my hands, Jack," Lawrence said. "The director wants to make an example of this case. Once it's known the Sample family is involved it's fodder for 20/20."

"Who's gonna play you?" Jane said.

"It's a mistake, Paul," I said.

"I follow orders, Jack, just like everybody else," Lawrence said.

"The Sample family isn't going to like the publicity," I said.

"Can't be helped," Lawrence said. "The boss wants what he wants."

"The boss is a moron," Jane said.

"Maybe so, but he's still the boss," Lawrence said.

"Let's order," I said.

"I hope crow is on the menu," Jane said, looking at Lawrence.

# Chapter Forty-four

I drove us to the Sample warehouse in Yonkers where an FBI SUV with three agents in it was parked in guest parking.

"Reinforcements?" I said.

"I don't like it anymore than you do," Lawrence said. "And I don't like having my friends act like my enemies, either."

"We both know what it's like having the brass breath down the back of your neck, Paul," I said.

"I know," Lawrence said.

"Are they going in with us?" I said and nodded to the three agents. "That kind of show of force will likely cause him to clam up tight."

"Just us three," Lawrence said. "But if we take him we go in my car."

\* \* \*

"What's this about?" Ludin said when he entered the conference room.

"We have some follow up questions," Lawrence said.

Ludin looked at Jane. "Who's she?" he said.

"My partner," I said.

"What questions?" Ludin said. "I already told you everything I know."

"Have a seat," Lawrence said. "Jack."

Ludin sat at the table while I worked the television and DVD player.

I watched his face to gauge his reaction when he saw what was on the DVD. The shock of seeing the strip club registered off the scale on his face.

"What is…?" he said.

"There. Right there," I said and hit pause.

Ludin closed his eyes.

"You lied to us, Chuck," Lawrence said. "You said you never saw Miss Bubbles before the night of the bachelor party and here we have you on ten of her DVDs."

"I can explain," Ludin said.

"And we'd love to hear it," Lawrence said.

"It's embarrassing for a guy to admit he spends so much time in a strip club," Ludin said.

"Not so much you haven't been back since Bubbles got together with Wally Sample," Lawrence said.

Ludin looked at me, then at Lawrence.

"Your friend there, Bo Dorn, have you seen him lately?" Lawrence said.

"Do I need a lawyer?" Ludin said.

"Do you want one?" Lawrence said.

"Yes."

"Then we have to go for a ride," Lawrence said.

"A ride? Where?" Ludin said.

"Manhattan. FBI regional office," Lawrence said.

"Aw come on," Ludin said.

"We can avoid all that by simply talking to us here and now," Lawrence said.

I watched the gears go round and round in Ludin's mind as he weighed his options. "No," he said. "I want a lawyer."

"Alright," Lawrence said. "Let's go for a ride."

*　　*　　*

We watched as Lawrence loaded Ludin into the back of the FBI SUV.

"This is not going to end well," Jane said.

"No."

"We might as well go home," Jane said.

"I'd like to stay another day," I said.

"What for? You know Ludin is going to walk and that ends any chance of finding the gorilla and the stripper," Jane said.

"You've been away a day longer than expected, so you should go home," I said. "I'm staying one more day."

"And miss the hot tub?" Jane said. "Let me call my office."

*　　*　　*

I grabbed a workout at the gym while Jane had a massage at the spa. Then we met at the pool where we soaked in the hot tub.

"That kid's lawyer will have him out of there in an hour," Jane said. "He'll clam up and that will be the end of it barring some miracle."

"Don't sell Paul short, he's a good cop and knows what he's doing," I said.

"He was a good cop," Jane said. "Now he's *F. B. I.* That's a different animal."

"What did you bring for evening wear?" I said.

# Chapter Forty-five

Charles Ludin lived in a crummy, four-story walk-up apartment building in Yonkers a few blocks from the old racetrack.

Jane and I sat in the rental with cups of takeout coffee. She lit a cigarette, took a hit and passed it to me.

I inhaled deeply and passed the cigarette back to Jane.

"You're a bad influence on me," I said.

"I hope so," Jane said. "How long are we going to sit here in the dark?"

"Until he shows," I said.

"I have to pee," Jane said. "All this coffee."

I handed Jane my empty coffee cup. "Hop in the back," I said.

"For God's sake," Jane said.

"You're a cop, remember?" I said. "When we're working you're not a woman and I'm not a man. We're partners."

"A real partner would have something better than a coffee cup," Jane said.

Next time I'll bring a bedpan," I said.

"How sweet," Jane said as she hopped in back.

\* \* \*

Jane was dozing with her head against her window when a Manhattan cab arrived and stopped in front of Ludin's building.

I nudged her and she was instantly awake.

"Ludin?" she said.

"He just showed up," I said.

Ludin exited the cab and walked to his building. Jane and I left the car and ran across the street and caught Ludin before he unlocked the lobby door to his building.

"Hello, Chuck," I said.

Ludin spun around, looked at me and gasped loudly. "What do you want?" he said.

"Talk," I said.

"I don't have to talk to you or anybody else," Ludin said.

He reeked of fear,

"No?" I said.

"No. Now please stop bothering me or I will call the police," Ludin said.

"Chuck, you're in so far over your head you're drowning," I said. "I'm your lifeline. Turn your back on me and I predict you'll be dead inside of forty-eight hours."

Ludin looked at Jane.

She nodded. "He speaks the truth, Chuck," she said.

"Come upstairs," Ludin said.

\*　\*　\*

Ludin's one-bedroom apartment was actually pretty neat and clean. He made a pot of coffee and we sat at the kitchen table with mugs of fresh brew.

"How did it go with the FBI?" I said.

"I refused to talk. I demanded a lawyer. They kept me in a room with no air for eight hours until a lawyer showed up. I had to piss in a coffee can. They had no choice but to let me go once the lawyer ripped into them," Ludin said.

"You'll be under surveillance from now on," I said. "Everywhere you go there they will be. The only question is how soon before Bo Dorn kills you."

Ludin removed a pack of cigarettes from his shirt pocket and lit one.

"Smoking is bad for you, Chuck," Jane said as she lit one of her own.

Ludin grinned at Jane. She winked at him as she took a sip of coffee.

"How did it happen?" I said. "From the beginning."

Ludin inhaled on his cigarette and I noticed his hands shook a bit. "I never met Bo before he came to work at the warehouse," he said. "We hit it off and he suggested we go out one night. I rarely have anything to do, so I went with him. He took me to the Cupid's Retreat and introduced me to his girlfriend."

"Bubbles," I said.

"He insisted I keep going with him and he's not somebody to say no to," Ludin said. "He scares the hell out of me."

"How did the whole kidnapping thing come about?" I said.

"One day about four or five months ago, Bo knocks on my door and he's got Bubbles with him," Ludin said. "Bo tells me they have a can't miss plan that will make them rich and he'll pay me one hundred thousand for helping them."

"To set up Wally with Bubbles?" I said.

Ludin nodded. "I made the call and arranged for her to do her show at the bachelor party and that's all I did," he said. "Bo quit after that and Bubbles took up with Wally. I knew they were going to fleece him but I had no idea about the kidnapping thing until you showed up asking questions. I thought maybe they would take a video of Wally in bed with her, something like that. That's the truth."

"Did you get your money?" I said.

"The deal was six months after the party I would get paid," Ludin said.

"He has no intentions of paying you," I said. "He'll show up one night soon and kill you and think nothing of it."

"I think you are right," Ludin said.

"You know he's right," Jane said.

"They played you for s sucker and can't afford to leave you alive to testify against them," I said.

"In other words, you're fucked," Jane said.

"What if I confessed?" Ludin said.

"For your part in an extortion scheme you might get eighteen months," I said. "Do you know where Dorn and Bubbles are?"

"No," Ludin said. "They could be anywhere."

"He'll either get to you in prison or when you get out," I said. "But if I can get you a deal with the feds in exchange for testimony you'll be protected for life."

"Change my name and all that like in the movies?" Ludin said.

"A lot of men take the deal. It beats being dead," Jane said.

"That other girl, Jackie, do you know her?" I said.

Ludin shook his head. "No, why?" he said.

"Doesn't matter," I said. "Should I call the FBI and get this over with?"

"Do I have a choice?" Ludin said.

I used my cell phone to call Lawrence.

"When are you headed back to D.C.?" I said.

"In the morning," he said.

"You might want to delay that," I said.

# Chapter Forty-six

Lawrence sat at the kitchen table opposite Ludin as Ludin wrote his statement.

Jane and I stood against the counter and watched.

"That's everything," Ludin said. "All of it."

Lawrence read the statement. "Here is what is going to happen, Mr. Ludin," he said. "You'll spend the night with us in Manhattan and the we'll take you to Washington tomorrow to meet someone from the Justice Department."

Ludin nodded.

Lawrence stood and looked at his men in the living room. Three men entered the kitchen. "Go with them now," Lawrence said.

"What about all my belongings?" Ludin said.

"They will be put in storage," Lawrence said.

Ludin nodded and left the kitchen with the three agents.

"I swear, Jack," Lawrence said.

"How does that crow taste, Paul?" Jane said.

Lawrence sighed.

"If you'll excuse me I have to use the bathroom," Jane said.

I looked at my watch. It was three in the morning.

"Want to find a place to get an early breakfast?" I said.

Jane returned and said, "Seeing as how we skipped dinner, my vote is yes."

* * *

"Can this place be any brighter?" Jane said.

We found a Denny's on Central Avenue in Yonkers where we ordered breakfast.

"We'll backtrack Ludin's statement and see if we can come up with a starting point for Dorn," Lawrence said. "Where he lived, his hangouts, his family, friends, whatever. He'll be put under a microscope until we turn something up."

"Ludin said the plan was to pay him in six months," I said. "If that's accurate Dorn is planning to move the bonds in four to five months. I don't think he'll sit on the bonds that long. I think sitting on fifteen million he can't spend is burning a hole in his pockets."

"If he cashes in those bonds we'll know about it," Lawrence said.

I looked at Jane and she shrugged.

"What?" Lawrence said.

"Your assuming he still has them," Jane said.

"I don't think Dorn is smart enough to play with the big boys," I said. "In fact, I think they already moved the bonds for say ten million to someone who is smart enough."

"God I hope you're wrong, Jack," Lawrence said.

"What's in Dorn's record that says he's this smart?" I said.

Lawrence stared at me for a moment. "You think Wilcox is the brains?" he said.

"From the very beginning," I said. "She wanted out but with money. She met Dorn at the club, won him over and knew he would do whatever she told him to. When Ludin entered the picture, she gradually formatted a plan to get to Wally. It was dumb luck that book fell into her lap and gave them a blueprint for the kidnapping."

"She still would need a mover and shaker to handle the bonds," Lawrence said.

"When we were in that club, do you know what I saw?" I said.

"A bunch of horny men wasting their money on women who wouldn't give them the time of day on the street," Jane said.

"Besides that," I said.

Lawrence and Jane looked at me.

"A lot of men in their twenties and thirties wearing suits," I said. "Who wears suits to a strip club?"

"Guys just getting off work," Jane said.

"Who wears suits to work?" I said.

"Lawyers, businessmen and… men who work in the financial district," Lawrence said.

"She cozied up to a stock broker or financial analyst and the next thing he knows he's kneed deep in bearer bonds, for a nice cut of course," I said.

"It fits," Lawrence said.

"You know what, check the NYPD stats for young stock brokers and analysts recently found murdered or not found at all," I said. "Dorn isn't going to part with any of the fifteen million if he doesn't have to."

"You think he would really kill him?" Lawrence said.

"I think Dorn would kill his grandmother for a quarter," I said. I closed my eyes for a moment, then they snapped open. "Damn," I said.

"What?" Jane said.

"The girl. Jackie," I said.

"You don't think he would…?" Lawrence said.

"It's worth checking out," I said.

"Now?" Jane said.

"She gets off after one, she's probably still awake," I said.

*   *   *

208

I parked on the street opposite Jackie's Queens apartment.

"6B," I said.

"And we know this how>" Jane said.

"Yell at me later," I said as I tried her number on my cell phone. It rang six times before her voice mailbox picked up.

I got out of the car, followed by Lawrence and Jane.

"6B would be facing the street," I said and counted windows. "Her lights are on."

We went to the lobby. The outer door was locked. I tried her number again with the same results.

There was one bell with an intercom beside the door. It was to the building superintendent. I pushed the bell and held it for a count of ten. I released the bell, waited five seconds and rang it again for another count of ten.

A gruff, sleepy voice spoke over the intercom. "The building better be on fire," he said.

"This is the FBI," Lawrence said. "We need to speak with you immediately."

"Who?" the voice said.

"FBI," Lawrence said. "Come to the lobby."

"Hold on," the voice said.

Two minutes passed and the superintendent appeared wearing a robe. Lawrence held his identification up to the glass, lobby door.

The superintendent buzzed us in.

"What's this about?" he said.

"Do you have a pass key for 6B?" Lawrence said.

"Sure."

"Get it," Lawrence said.

A few minutes later, the superintendent unlocked the door to 6B.

"Stay in the hall," Lawrence said.

We entered the apartment. Lights were on in every room. We

checked the living room and kitchen and went to the bedroom.

I didn't need a doctor to see Jackie was dead.

Lawrence took out his cell phone and called 911.

\* \* \*

Lawrence and a New York City detective chatted while a ME team removed Jackie's body from the apartment.

It was obvious that Jackie had been choked to death by a pair of extremely powerful hands.

The kind of hands a Bo Dorn possesses.

"Why kill her?" Jane said. "She couldn't have harmed Dorn or Wilcox."

"She was a loose thread in the plan," I said. "She knew about the book and she identified Ludin and Dorn on the DVDs."

"Horrible way to die," Jane said.

"This means Dorn is still relatively close, or was," I said. "Close enough to keep an eye on things."

Lawrence broke away from the detective. "We're done here," he said.

"Did the ME say how long she's been dead?" I said.

"At least twenty-four hours," Lawrence said.

"Thirty-six hours ago, Jane and I spoke to her at the club," I said. "For all we know he was there watching."

"Creepy," Jane said.

"Sun's up," I said. ""I need some sleep. Call me later, Paul."

\* \* \*

I slept for six hours and left Jane in bed and hit the hotel gym for a workout. I did some weights, push-ups and sit-ups and then ran on a treadmill for about an hour to clear my mind.

Jackie, an innocent bystander was dead and Ludin was in Federal custody. Lawrence was probably still asleep or sleeping on a plane back to Washington.

Wally was still at my house, but should be able to go home soon.

Bo Dorn and Barbara Wilcox could be anywhere by now if they cashed in the bonds.

There's that word again.

If.

I knew Bo Dorn's type. He enjoyed violence. He enjoyed hurting others and even killing. His ego wouldn't allow him to use a gun or knife. He took fierce pride in his size and strength and got off on the fact he was the eight hundred pound gorilla in the room.

Seeing men cower in his presence fed his ego even more and he never missed an opportunity to use his power to humiliate others.

After an hour, I toweled dry and was about to return to the room when a thought flashed through my mind and I pulled my cell phone from the pocket of my warm-up pants and called Lawrence.

"You awake?" I said.

"The manager," I said.

"What?"

"Of the Cupid's Retreat," I said. "He's the one who found the book and gave it to me. If Dorn knew about Jackie he knows about Dorn."

"I'll meet you in the lobby in one hour," Lawrence said.

\* \* \*

Lawrence used his clout with NYPD to track down the manager's address. I drove us to a small home near Kennedy Airport, It was one of a dozen homes on a block that nobody wanted to live on but the prices of the homes were too cheap to pass on.

We met two police cruisers in front of the house.

Two uniformed officers used a door spreader to open the heavyweight, Oak door and we filed in.

The manager was dead in his easy chair. His neck was broken, snapped like a dry chicken bone.

Dorn was removing his loose ends.

Lawrence sighed openly. "Fuck," he said.

It was that kind of morning.

# Chapter Forty-seven

By the time the ME cleared the body and NYPD dusted and searched for forensics, it was after one in the afternoon.

I drove us back to White Plains where we had lunch at the hotel.

"Dorn and Wilcox go on the FBI most wanted list as of today," Lawrence said.

"At least he didn't get Ludin," I said.

"True, but without Dorn or Wilcox in custody he's of no real value to us," Lawrence said.

"Anything on the bonds? Any dead brokers?" I said.

"Nothing yet," Lawrence said.

"So he's sitting on fifteen million without a way to move them," I said. "He must be pretty steamed."

"I've head enough of this guy and his stripper," Jane said. "Jack, it's time to go home."

"She's right," Lawrence said. "You've done everything possible and more. Now we wait until somebody somewhere picks him up or he screws up. Either way, ho home."

\* \* \*

"We should have used the hot tub one more time before we left," Jane said.

Our plane had just landed and we were taxing to our gate.

"Next time," I said.

Once we were off the plane, retrieved out luggage and made our way to the parking lot it was close to sundown.

When we walked through the front door of my house, Oz was reading a book in his easy chair while Regan and Wally played a video game.

They stopped what they were doing and came to greet us, along with Cuddles and Molly.

"How was your vacation?" Oz said.

"Illuminating," I said. "Let's celebrate our return by going out to dinner."

\*     \*     \*

Wally ordered salad, a small bowl of soup and a baked chicken breast with vegetables.

"Tell him, Wally," Regan said.

"I did two miles today, And twelve push-ups and fifteen sit-ups and I've lost nine pounds," Wally said.

"Tomorrow we'll do our workout and then hit the beach," I said.

"I have to work," Regan said.

"Oz will go," I said.

"I'll go but I ain't walking no two miles," Oz said.

"I have to get back to the office," Jane said.

"I guess it's just the three of us," I said.

\*     \*     \*

Jane was silent next to me in the day bed, It was after midnight and we should have been asleep.

"Bekker?" Jane said softly.

"Yeah?"

She sat up and reached for the lamp beside the daybed and turned it on. "I'm having a cigarette," Jane said, got up and reached into her bag.

After she lit a cigarette, I sat up and looked at her.

"This creep is bugging me," Jane said. "All that money, two murders, a headless corpse and he's out there free with his bimbo."

"It could be quite a while before he turns up," I said. "Bulger was on the FBI Most Wanted list for sixteen years and it was only a fluke he was ever captured."

Jane handed me the cigarette and I inhaled and gave it back to her.

"How was he keeping tabs on things?" I said.

Jane blew a smoke ring at the ceiling. "Probably by visiting the strip club," she said.

"I don't think so," I said. "His size sticks out like a second thumb. He wouldn't risk being remembered in public."

"A friend?" Jane said.

"This guy kills his friends," I said.

"So what's your theory?" Jane said.

"Barbara get her breasts reduced back to her normal size, dyes her hair back to redhead and comes and goes freely," I said. "I saw women alone or with other women in the club and she would be invisible."

"She might have even saw us when we talked to Jackie and the manager," Jane said.

"That's what I'm thinking," I said.

"That little bitch rats us out to Dorn and he kills the both of them," Jane said.

"It fits," I said.

"But they still don't have the money," Jane said. "I hope they choke on it."

Jane handed me the cigarette. I took another hit and then put it out in the coffee cup beside the lamp.

"Let's get some sleep," I said.

Jane removed her tank top. "I have a better idea," she said.

# Chapter Forty-eight

After a breakfast of oatmeal with blueberries and two slices of buttered toast, orange juice and coffee, Jane left for work.

Shortly after that, Regan left for her job at the pet store.

"Okay, Wally, let's change," I said.

A few minutes later, we met in the backyard. We started with push-ups, sit-ups and pull-ups, some rope jumping and then I switched to weights.

We ended with work on the heavy and speed bags.

Then Oz joined us for the drive to the beach. Oz chose a spot to open his folding chair and sit and read while Wally and I started our walk.

"Some things I want to discuss with you," I said.

Wally looked up at me. "Okay."

I told him about Bo Dorn, Jackie and the manager of the strip club. "The thing is, Wally, I don't think he's found a way to convert the bonds to cash as yet," I said. "I don't think it's safe for you to go home yet."

"I can't keep living in your bedroom, Mr. Bekker," Wally said.

"For now you're safe," I said. "If you go home, he'll get to you. One way or another, he'll get to you."

"I could hire a bodyguard," Wally said.

"That won't stop him," I said. "He go after your family if he can't get to you. This guy is evil. I've seen his handiwork and it's not pretty."

"What else can I do?" Wally said. "I can't hide forever and I can't risk my family."

"I have an idea but I'll tell you about it later," I said. "Let's see if you can sprint to Oz."

We sprinted the last hundred yards to Oz where Wally collapsed at Oz's feet, got on his back and wheezed loudly.

Oz looked at me. "What's wrong with you? You trying to kill this knucklehead?"

I sat beside Wally and looked at the ocean. "That developer should be ready to take deposits soon," I said.

"I'll give him a call tomorrow," Oz said.

"Wally, are you ready to go home?" I said.

Wally sat up. "I'm ready," he said. "But first I think I have to puke."

*   *   *

I sat at the patio table in my backyard with a can of ginger ale and my cell phone.

I called Lawrence in Washington. "How is Ludin holding up?" I said.

"About what you'd expect," Lawrence said. "If he knew anything more he would have spilled his guts by now."

"I have a theory," I said. "Care to hear it?"

"All ears, Jack."

"Barbara Wilcox got a breast reduction, dyed her hair back to redhead and became Dorn's eyes and ears at the club," I said. "There were women at the club, she could have been one of them. She could have been there when we were and told tales out of school to Dorn."

"That fits, Jack," Lawrence said. "Like an old shoe."

"It means while we were spinning our wheels they were close," I said. "And my guess is they still are."

"Sitting on those bonds must be making them crazy," Lawrence said.

"Crazy enough to make them make a mistake," I said.

"Let's hope so," Lawrence said.

After Lawrence, I called Jane. She was on duty in her office.

"I'm working a double, Jack," she said. "All things considered I'd rather be in the hot tub."

"All things considered, me too," I said.

"You better buy me a ring, soon, Jack," Jane said. "I'm sick of this damn job plenty."

"You trust my judgment?"

"Nope."

"I'll get a saleswoman to help me."

"Good idea."

After hanging up with Jane, Regan came out to the backyard and sat next to me at the patio table.

"Pot roast in fifteen minutes," she said.

"Thank you, honey," I said.

"Dad, how long is Wally going to stay with us?" Regan said.

"I know it's a burden, honey, but—" I said.

"No, Dad, it's not," Regan said. "I feel like I have a big brother. Somebody I can talk to and relate to. I was afraid to ask this and he encouraged me."

"Ask what?"

"Having Tony over to dinner."

"I don't see why not," I said.

"Thanks, Dad. I'm thinking Saturday."

"Saturday it is," I said.

"I better check the pot roast," Regan said.

"Wait. How long do you want Wally to stay?"

"As long as he wants," Regan said. "Or until you get sick or sleeping in the basement."

# Chapter Forty-nine

A week passed without any movement from Dorn or Wilcox. They must be stewing in their own juices over their lack of ability to exchange the bonds.

I worked out in the backyard and went for walks on the beach with Wally and Regan when she wasn't at the pet store.

I spent a lot of time with Jane when she wasn't working. I worked up the courage to shop for rings. I took my time and visited several jewelry stores. I hadn't found what I wanted but at least I had a general idea.

I met with Frank Kagan to discuss a few possible corporate investigations.

Dinner with Tony was an experience. A more nervous, gawky boy I never did meet. Regan liked him and for now that was enough.

Oz made an appointment to meet with the real estate developer and we went to his office to look at units.

By next summer we would have a condo on the beach. It wasn't a trailer and we would have neighbors, but nothing is perfect.

I spent a lot of time at my desk, checking my case notes, hoping that some detail would emerge and reveal that final piece of the puzzle and lead me to Dorn and Wilcox.

It didn't.

We held a backyard barbecue and invited Jane, Walt and his wife Elizabeth and Tony. I cooked up a mess of ribs, burgers, dogs and steak tips with baked potatoes and beans and it wasn't like the cookouts we used to have at the beach, but it was close.

In a private moment, I brought Walt up to par on the investigation.

"Sounds like you did everything possible," Walt said.

"Except catch the bad guys," I said.

"Knowing you, you're not done with it yet," Walt said.

I wasn't.

And they weren't done with me either.

\* \* \*

On a nice Monday morning, I met with Frank Kagan in his office. Since his day of representing mobster Eddie Crist, he had gone completely legit and found he was enjoying practicing civil law.

He had some insurance work for me. Fraudulent claims. The money was good. I took the file folders home to study them.

A car was parked in the driveway in front of the closed garage, It had rental plates on it.

The hairs on the back of my neck stood up. Mt glove box was equipped with a lock and I used the key to unlock it and I removed the .357 Magnum revolver I keep in it for emergency use.

I tucked the .357 into my belt and buttoned my suit jacket.

The front door was unlocked and I entered my home. The television was on and someone was watching cartoons.

Oz and Regan were on the sofa, their hands and ankles bound with duct tape. A strip of tape covered their mouth.

Barbara Wilcox was in Oz's recliner. She was eating a bowl of Cheerios and watching cartoons.

Without looking at me, she said, "Come in, Mr. Bekker."

I walked to Barbara and she grinned at me. She set the bowl on Oz's tray table and used the remote to mute the television. "We got the little retard," she said.

Oz and Regan looked at me with eyes as wide as silver dollars.

"You wasted your time," I said. "Wally wouldn't have a clue how to cash in those bonds."

"No, but *you* do," Barbara said. "Have a seat. Please."

I sat beside Oz.

"I told Bo the moment I saw you that first time you came into the club you would be trouble," Barbara said.

She had cut and dyed her hair red and her breasts were several sizes smaller inside her tank top.

"I told him money but he knew this financial guy who deals in bonds," Barbara said.

"Knew?" I said.

"He wouldn't cooperate," Barbara said.

"What makes you think I will?" I said. "You didn't take my daughter or Oz; you took a stranger."

"A man doesn't go to all the trouble you did for a stranger," Barbara said. "Living in your house, runs on the beach, very cozy."

"He hired me," I said.

"We know. We took your business card from Jackie's apartment," Barbara said. "It's amazing what you can find using a phone number."

"The man who took the body from the hospital, who was he?" I said.

"An old friend who worked there," Barbara said. "Don't worry, he's no longer in the picture."

"I want guarantees," I said.

"Then buy a fucking toaster and fill out the little card," Barbara said.

"You're a very smart girl, Barbara," I said. "Too smart to not realize that when Dorn gets the money he'll kill you too."

Barbara grinned at me. She had the look in her eyes and grin of a woman not all there. She reminded me of the crazed woman in the opening scene of the movie Pulp Fiction.

"Bo loves me," Barbara said. "When he told me about the little retard I just knew we could play this and I could finally walk away from those perverts and their dollar bills."

"Nobody forced you to become a stripper," I said.

"Stripper is so old school," Barbara said. "Exotic dancer is what we're called these days."

Barbara picked up the bowl of Cheerios and ate a spoonful. "On your bed you'll find the bonds," he said. "You have one week to cash them in if you want the retard returned to you in one piece."

"Who's to say I won't keep them for myself?" I said.

"Bo would kill that old man and your kid if you attempted that," Barbara said. "So be smart, cash the bonds and then call the number we left with the bonds when you have the money. We get what we want and you get what you want."

"I won't do a damn thing unless Wally is alive," I said.

"After I leave, call the number," Barbara said.

She set the bowl on the tray, stood up and walked out. I grabbed a knife from the kitchen and cut the tape from Oz and Regan and they ripped off the tape.

"I come out the bathroom and this big son of a bitch holding Regan," Oz said. "The girl had a gun to Wally's head."

I hugged Regan. "Are you alright?" I said.

Instead of fear in Regan's eyes, I saw fuming anger. "You're not going to let them get away with this, are you?" she said.

"First things first," I said.

I went to my bedroom where a leather covered, wood briefcase was on the bed. The phone number was scrawled on the briefcase in red lipstick.

I called the number.

Bo Dorn answered. "Can't wait to meet cha," he said.

"Likewise," I said.

"You got one week like she said," Dorn said. "After that, the retard dies and then I come for your family. The cops won't be able to protect them. Do we understand each other?"

"Yes. Let me talk to Wally," I said.

After a few seconds, Wally said, "Mr. Bekker."

"Sit tight, Wally. I'll get you out of this," I said. "And don't do anything stupid. Just do what he says."

"Okay, Mr. Bekker," Wally said.

Dorn came back on the line. "One week," he said and hung up.

# Chapter Fifty

I sat in the backyard at the patio table and drank a mug of coffee. My mind was in overdrive, so much so I didn't hear Regan until she was next to me at the table.

"What are you doing?" she said.

"Thinking," I said.

"I've seen you so drunk you couldn't stand up," Regan said. "I've seen you beat up, stabbed and shot, but I've never seen you quit."

"I'm not quitting now," I said.

"They'll kill Wally," Regan said.

"No they won't," I said. "They know before I release the money I'll want to talk to him."

"Just get him back, Dad," Regan said.

I nodded.

"I'd like to punch that bitch right in the nose," Regan said.

Likewise. "Can you get Oz for me?" I said.

Regan nodded and went inside.

Oz came out and took a chair at the table.

"Do still have that shotgun?" I said.

"The Greener? Sure do," Oz said.

"Keep it with you and make sure it's loaded," I said. "If anybody except me or Jane comes to the door, give them both barrels."

"Fucking right," Oz said.

"I'll be back," I said.

\* \* \*

The Crist mansion wasn't far, maybe forty-five minutes away. It sat on a hill and was surrounded by a tall, black-iron fence.

A guard shack was on the other side of the fence. The guard inside called up to the house and then opened the gate and allowed me to pass.

Carly Simms greeted me at the door with a hug and kiss. "This is a surprise, come in," she said.

Campbell Crist was in the large living room where the baby sat in a crib.

"I thought I smelled the aroma of man," Campbell said.

"Be nice," Carly said.

"I'm here, hat in hand, to beg a favor," I said.

"You don't have a hat," Campbell said.

The baby started to cry.

"Carly, please," Campbell said.

Carly picked up the baby and sat beside Campbell. "It wouldn't hurt you to pick him up once in a while," she said.

"And get drool on my silk blouse?" Campbell replied.

"What favor?" Carly asked.

I spent the next twenty minutes explaining the situation to them and ended with, "Can you put them up until this is over?"

"What happens if you get killed?" Campbell said.

"Then you can keep them both," I said.

"Great, just what I've always wanted, an eighty-year-old Black grandfather and a twenty-year-old step-daughter," Campbell said.

"For God's sake, Campbell," Carly said.

"Can they stay with you until I clear this up or not?" I asked.

"Of course they can, you dense blockhead of a man," Campbell replied.

"I'll be back shortly," I said.

"Toodles," Campbell said.

\* \* \*

"What about you, Dad, you'll be all alone?" Regan said.

"And if I don't have to worry about you and Oz, I can concentrate of getting Wally back," I said.

We arrived at the gate to the Crist mansion.

"So this how the other half live, huh?" Oz said.

I drove past the open gate to the house.

Carly greeted us at the door. She hugged Regan and kissed Oz on the cheek.

Oz looked around as we followed Carly to the living room.

Campbell stood up from the sofa and gave Regan a hug. "Thank God you don't look like your dad," she said.

"Regan, you have the bedroom at the end of the second floor hall," Carly said. "Oz, we have a room on the first floor for you."

"Because we don't want you having a heart attack climbing the stairs," Campbell said.

"Can't you for once be delicate?" Carly said.

"It's true," Campbell said.

The baby started to cry and Regan said, "Can I?"

"Please do, because I won't," Campbell said. "It's bad enough the little crying machine sleeps in our room."

Regan lifted the baby in her arms and the crying stopped.

"Stay for dinner?" Carly said to me.

"Can't," I said. "Too much to do."

"Dad, be careful," Regan said.

"Don't worry," I said. "Ladies, thank you."

"Thanks for the baby sitter," Campbell said.

# Chapter Fifty-one

"This fucking guy! I'm going to blow his stupid brains out," Jane said. "And make Barbara Wilcox clean them up with a spoon."

I handed Jane a cup of coffee and she lit a cigarette.

"What did Lawrence and Walt say about all this?"

I took the chair at the patio table to Jane's left. "I haven't told them yet."

"Are you crazy? Why not?"

"Because I don't want to get Wally killed," I said.

"Do you know anything about those bonds?" Jane said.

"Not a thing," I said. "But I know someone who dies."

"I have to work, but I'll stay over until this is resolved," Jane said. "And then I'm going to take a shotgun to the oversize asshole."

"First things first," I said. "Regan and Oz are safe, so the main focus now is Wally."

"And you don't want to bring in Walt or Paul?" Jane said.

"Not yet," I said. "Not until I get this figured out."

"It's after seven, want something to eat?"

"Yeah, I'll fix something."

"While you do that, I'm going for a shower," she said.

There were a pair of nice steaks in the fridge and I fired up the grill and tossed them on, along with some potatoes. Jane came out wearing one of my long-sleeve shirts, shorts and slippers.

228

"Say you convert the bonds, you just going to hand this asshole fifteen million?" she said.

"Not hand, exchange," I said.

"Provided Wally is still alive," Jane said.

"He wants the money," I said. "Wally dead doesn't get him that."

"Maybe, but I still think you should call Paul," Jane said.

"I will. Just not yet," I said.

"Those steaks ready?"

"Just about."

*   *   *

"So, this is a real bed," Jane said as she snuggled against my chest.

"The day bed isn't that bad," I said. "In fact, I kind of enjoyed the illegal midnight visits."

"This place feels empty without Regan and Oz," Jane said.

Cuddles and Molly jumped onto the bed and settled near our feet.

"I spoke too soon," Jane said.

"If they crawl on top of you, just kick them off," I said.

"Bekker, where do you think they have Wally?" Jane said.

"Hard to say," I said. "A rented apartment. A motel. Wherever they have him, it's close. No more than two hours from here."

"Jack, Paul has the—"

"Paul and the FBI will want to negotiate for Wally's release," I said. "You can't negotiate with a psychopath like Dorn. All that will get you is dead, and a dead Wally defeats the purpose."

"And you?"

"I can take care of myself," I said.

"Remember the first time you met Wally?" Jane said.

"This is different," I said.

"Yeah? How? One psychopath is the same as another."

"I admit I have my quirks, but I don't think I measure up to psychopath status," I said.

Jane jabbed me in the ribs. "Go to sleep," she said.

\* \* \*

A bit after 3:00 in the morning, I woke up, untangled myself from Jane's legs, and went to the kitchen. The nightlight was on but I switched on the small light above the stove. Then I filled a glass with milk and removed a bag of chocolate chip cookies from a cabinet and sat at the table.

I dunked a cookie into the milk and took a bite.

A few moments later, wearing one of my white dress shirts, Jane wandered into the kitchen. "What are you doing?" she said.

"Having cookies and milk," I said.

Jane filled a glass with milk and sat next to me. She grabbed a cookie, dunked it and took a bite.

"Now tell me what you're really doing," Jane said.

"Thinking," I said.

Jane ate the rest of her cookie. "Does it hurt?" she said.

"Sometimes," I said.

"So what are you really thinking?"

"That if I screw this up Wally is dead and possibly me as well," I said.

"So don't screw it up," Jane said.

She grabbed another cookie, dunked it in her milk and ate half of it. She looked at the bag. "One hundred and fifty calories for two cookies, are you kidding me?" she said.

"Do you know what happens if I call Paul?" I said.

"Yeah. Wally will be negotiated to death," Jane said. "Let's go back to bed. I need to work off these cookie calories."

# Chapter Fifty-two

I dumped the briefcase on Kagan's desk. "I need help," I said.

Kagan stood, opened the briefcase and looked at the bonds. "My oh my," he said.

"Never mind my oh my," I said. "How do I cash them legally?"

Kagan looked at me. "How much do we like Wally?" he said.

"Frank," I said.

"Just kidding," Kagan said and closed the briefcase. "We need a commercial bank willing to cash them. A regular bank wouldn't do."

"Hold onto the briefcase, I'll be right back," I said.

I went to the hallway and used my cell phone to call Robert Sample.

"Mr. Bekker, what can I…?" he said.

"No time. Just listen," I said. "Bo Dorn and Barbara Wilcox broke into my house when I wasn't there and kidnapped Wally. They want me to convert the bonds to cash to buy him back. I have six days."

"Jesus Christ these people," Robert said.

"Send your private jet for me first thing in the morning and then take me to your commercial bank to cash the bonds," I said.

"I'll have to call them," Robert said.

"Call them. Set it up for tomorrow afternoon," I said.

"Is Wally okay?" Robert said.

"Yes, and I'd like to keep him that way," I said.

"I'll send the plane tonight for an early take off in the morning," Robert said.

"Thank you. I'll be there. And don't worry, I'll get Wally back," I said.

After hanging up, I returned to Kagan's office.

"We're flying to New York tomorrow morning," I said. "You will act as Wally's attorney and oversee the transaction."

"I better call the airlines," Kagan said.

"The Sample private jet," I said. "I'll meet you at the airfield at seven am tomorrow morning."

"The last time I was on a private jet was before Crist died," Kagan said.

"See you in the morning," I said.

*   *   *

Jane watched as I hung the suit I was going to wear in the morning on the hook behind the bathroom door.

She was soaking in a tub full of bubble bath. A lit cigarette dangled from her lips.

"I can't go with you in the morning," Jane said. "Sheriff stuff."

"I'll be back before dinner time," I said.

"That big bastard Magnum I saw you put of the dresser, are you taking that?" Jane said.

"I'd hate to lose fifteen million now," I said.

"Are you getting in?" Jane said.

I stripped of my T-shirt and shorts and maneuvered my way around Jane and sat opposite her in the tub.

"I know you're working on a plan," Jane said. "I can see the little mice on their little wheel spinning away inside your head. What have you come up with so far?"

"Bring the money back safe," I said.

"Speaking of safe, it was nice of the ladies to give Oz and Regan sanctuary," Jane said.

"I owe them," I said.

"Not as much as they owe you," Jane said.

"Not important right now who owes who," I said. "Wally doesn't deserve any of what's happened to him and I have to make this right."

"We," Jane said. "We have to make this right. And if you ask Walt and Paul they would say the same thing."

"Not yet," I said. "I don't want to do anything that might get Wally killed."

Jane nodded. "I'm hungry," she said.

\* \* \*

I sat on the edge of my bed and called Regan's cell phone.

"How are you sweetheart?" I said.

"Did you know this place has a movie theatre and a bowling alley?" she said.

"Actually, I did know that," I said.

"Oz and I are going to bowl a few games after dinner," Regan said.

"Regan, call your boss and tell him you can't come in for a week," I said.

"Dad," Regan said.

"Regan, it's too dangerous," I said. "One week."

"Alright," Regan said.

"I'll talk to you later," I said.

I held the phone in my hand and watched Jane as she went through my closet and picked out one of my shirts to wear. She settled on a long-sleeve, button-down blue shirt.

I punched in the number Wilcox left. After three rings, she answered the phone.

"What can I do for you, Mr. Bekker?" she said.

"I am making arrangements to convert the bonds," I said. "I just want to make sure what I'm buying is still alive."

"Ten seconds," Wilcox said.

Wally came on the phone. "Mr. Bekker," he said.

"Are you okay?" I said.

"I'm not hurt," Wally said.

"Sit tight, listen to them and don't panic," I said.

"Time's up," Wilcox said. "Call back when you have the money."

I tossed the phone and looked at Jane as she brushed her hair in the mirror over the dresser.

"Why do women always look better in men's shirts than men do?" I said.

"That's a question for another time," Jane said. "Let's eat."

# Chapter Fifty-three

"Nice plane," Kagan said.

I brought two cups of coffee from the galley and set them on the table in from of Kagan.

"Breakfast in ten minutes," I said and took a chair.

Kagan took a sip of coffee. "How is Wally holding up?"

"He's alive," I said. "I spoke to him last night."

"How are Regan and the old man?"

"Safe with Campbell and Carly," I said.

"How old is Regan now?"

"Soon to be twenty," I said.

"My God, has it been three years since Crist passed away?" Kagan said.

"Just about," I said.

"When we first met you were a..." Kagan said.

"Drunk," I said.

"A heavy drinker," Kagan said. "Without focus or a plan for life."

"That's polite," I said. "Boozer would be more like it."

The microwave pinged and I went to the Galley. I returned with fried egg and bacon sandwiches, potato patties and orange juice.

"You've done all that you could and more to make up for it," Kagan said. "I, on the other hand have no avenue for redemption having served Satan for so long."

"You're helping to save Wally's life. That won't go unnoticed."

Kagan smiled at me. "Good sandwich," he said.

\* \* \*

Robert's limo was waiting for us at the airport.

"You must be Frank Kagan," Robert said.

Kagan and Robert shook hands. Then we entered the rear of the limo and the driver took us to Manhattan.

The rear seats of the limo held six and had a coffee bar in the middle. Robert made a pot of coffee for the hour-long drive.

"I made an appointment with the president of the bank," Robert said. "We've been doing business for twenty-five-years, so I expect a smooth transaction."

I held the briefcase in my lap. "Will this case hold fifteen million in cash?" I said.

"No, but I have one in the trunk that will," Robert said.

"Is your driver armed?" I said.

"Licensed and armed," Robert said. "Now, how is my brother?"

"I spoke to him last night," I said. "He sounded in good spirits."

"I fear that when this is over my brother will be set back quite a ways." Robert said.

"Don't sell Wally short," I said. "He's much tougher than you know."

"I hope so," Robert said.

We arrived at the bank on 6th Avenue near Rock Center forty-five minutes later. We were escorted by an armed guard to the bank manager's office.

"Mr. Franks, this is an attorney in this matter, Frank Kagan and Mr. Bekker," Robert said.

"I can't say as I've ever been involved in such a transaction before, but it's your money, Mr. Sample," Franks said.

Changing the bonds back to currency and recording the bonds

took two hours. By the time we returned to the jet it was after 5:00 in the afternoon.

We shook hands with Robert.

"Don't worry, Robert, we'll get Wally back alive," I said.

"I believe you," Robert said.

I looked at Kagan.

"Frank, let's go," I said.

\* \* \*

Jane greeted me at the front door, wearing one of my shirts and holding her Glock 26 in her right hand.

"I made dinner," Jane said. "Sort of. I burned it and ordered take out."

First things first. I went to the bedroom, set the large money bag on the floor, then removed my suit jacket and shoulder holster and tossed them on the bed.

Jane was heating up cartons of Chinese food in the microwave when I entered the kitchen.

I sat in a chair at the table.

"You look exhausted," Jane said.

"I am," I said.

"Have some food. We'll turn in early," Jane said.

I ate some noodles with chicken and broccoli.

"Regan called earlier. She said we're invited to dinner tomorrow night if we can make it," Jane said. "Can we make it?"

"Yes," I said. "We can make it. I'm going to let Dorn stew for a few days. I'll call and ask to talk to Wally in the morning."

"Jack, this is going to work out, isn't it?" Jane said.

"Sure," I said.

As soon as I figured out how.

# Chapter Fifty-four

"I'm okay, Mr. Bekker," Wally said. "They haven't hurt me."

"It won't be much longer, Wally," I said. "Stay strong and you'll be home before you know it."

"I will," Wally said.

Dorn suddenly came on the line. "We haven't hurt your little friend, Bekker and we won't if you come through with the money."

"I'll have it tomorrow," I said. "I'll deliver it to the place where I run on the beach at ten o'clock at night. I'll give you the money and you give me Wally."

"No cops. Just you," Dorn said. "I see anybody else and Wally dies. No matter what else happens, Wally dies. Are we clear on that?"

"Yes," I said.

"I can't wait to meet you, Bekker," Dorn said and hung up.

\*   \*   \*

I sat at my desk in the basement and made some phone calls. Then I went to the backyard where Molly and Cuddles were wrestling around on the grass.

I warmed up with the jump rope and then went right to the heavy bag. I worked the jab and combinations and let my thoughts go into a free-fall.

I lost track of time as I pounded the bag.

Every move, every detail no matter how minor had to be examined and thought out precisely or Wally could wind up dead and me along with him.

Dorn's ego was his weakness. The odds were he wouldn't be armed. He would want to kill me barehanded.

That didn't mean Wilcox wouldn't be armed. As I didn't want to get shot, she would have to be dealt with swiftly.

I lost track of how long I was working the bag. My arms grew weary and my shoulders ached and finally I lowered my hands.

I drank a bottle of water. Then I grabbed another bottle and drove to the beach. I parked in the municipal lot and walked to the sand. The tide was low, the waves gentle.

A few couples were walking their dogs, otherwise I was alone.

I jogged past the location where my trailer served as home for a decade. I ran for thirty minutes to the rocks and paused to drink some water.

He agreed to meet on the beach. They had to be close. I scaled the rocks and looked at another municipal parking lot. A few blocks away was a highway.

I descended the rocks and jogged back to my car.

The dog walkers were gone. I was alone.

Sometimes it's better that way.

\* \* \*

Campbell opened the front door, turned and said, "Bekker and the blonde are here."

Jane went ridged and was about to say something when I tugged on her arm to settle her down.

We followed Campbell to the formal dining room where Regan, Oz and Carly waited.

"Hello, Jane, nice to see you," Carly said.

Regan greeted me and Jane with a hug and kiss.

"Where's the baby?" I said.

"Sleeping," Carly said. "We have a monitor."

"Jane, I love what you've done with your hair," Campbell said.

"I haven't done anything to my hair," Jane said.

"I know," Campbell said.

Jane's nostrils flared, but I cut her off by pulling out a chair for her.

\*　\*　\*

After dinner, I had some time with Oz, Regan, and Jane in the massive backyard gardens.

The grass and flowers smelled sweet and fresh.

I sat in a lounge chair at the pool. The first time I met Eddie Crist in the flesh was at this very pool. He basically had me kidnapped and I was too damn drunk to do anything about it. After a grueling seventy-two hours detoxing on a bed in a room somewhere in the mansion, I met him poolside.

I wouldn't say we became friends after that, but I did develop a certain respect for the dying mobster. When he passed, I attended his funeral.

Regan sat on my lap and hugged me around the neck.

"Dad, you went away once," she said. "Bring Wally home, but promise me you won't go away again."

What else was there to do except promise?

# Chapter Fifty-five

Waiting has the ability to slow time to a crawl. Five minutes in a dentist chair can seem like an hour. A one hour layover at an airport can seem like a week. Most people are terrible at waiting.

When the light turns green, if you don't jump on the gas immediately the driver behind you honks the horn because he had to wait one whole second.

I once spent eighteen hours in a car, waiting to grab a photo of a mobster coming out of his apartment. The most difficult part of an assignment isn't falling asleep, it's losing focus.

Focus is everything. Lose focus for even one second and you miss the opportunity to take the photograph. Many a boxes lost a fight due to a fleeting moment where he lost focus.

The same could be said for any sport. Lose focus, lose the game.

After Jane left for work, I killed ninety minutes with a workout in the backyard. I didn't go for a run afterward because I wanted my legs to be strong for tonight.

I grilled a couple of burgers for lunch and ate at the patio table. Then I took a nap.

Sleeping is a good way to kill time.

I woke up around 4:30 and made a pot of coffee. I avoided going to the office as I didn't want emails or phone calls to distract me.

I watched a movie on television. It was one I hadn't seen before.

It was a remake of a classic western and although it wasn't as good, it held my attention.

I made some pasta with red sauce for dinner, but didn't eat too much.

I took a hot shower but didn't shave and put on a dark blue warm-up suite. Then I sat in the backyard and waited until it was time to leave.

At nine o'clock I took the money bag to the car and drove to the beach.

# Chapter Fifty-six

Walking from the municipal parking lot to the beach, the moon was bright enough to navigate the sand without a flashlight.

I carried the money bag in my right hand,

I walked to the area where my trailer used to sit, a distance of about three hundred yards, dropped the bag and waited.

The moon lit up the ocean well enough to see the waves crest and crash against the sand.

I was alone as far as I could tell. Except for the waves lashing out against the sand I couldn't see movement of any kind.

I waited.

Then, there it was.

Off in the distance, a pair of headlights broke through the darkness. They were too far off to hear an engine, but they grew larger as they advanced toward me.

It took about ten minutes for the golf cart to show up. Wilcox was driving. Bo Dorn was the passenger.

I picked up the money bag as they exited the cart.

"You must be Bekker," Dorn said.

"Is that the money?" Wilcox said.

"It is," I said.

About fifteen feet separated us.

"Show it to me," Dorn said.

I opened the zipper a bit, removed a stack of hundred dollar bills, and tossed it to Dorn. He rifled through the bills and pocketed them.

"Barbara, get the bag," Dorn said.

I took a step back. "Wally, first," I said.

"He's at the same number," Dorn said.

I took out my cell phone and punched in a series of numbers and then the cell phone for Wally.

It rang twice and Wally said, "Mr. Bekker?"

"It's me, Wally. Where are you?" I said.

"The Weary Traveler Inn off the highway," Wally said. "I'm handcuffed to the radiator."

"Sit tight," I said.

I hit the speaker button. "Jane, you hear that?"

"I did. Wally, I'm on the way," Jane said.

"Walt, Paul, did you get that?" I said.

"We did," Walt said.

"Come ahead," I said.

Dorn stared at me.

"What, you never heard of conference call?" I said.

Dorn looked in the distance as Jane's cruiser lit up.

"Barbara, get the money," Dorn said.

Wilcox pulled a pistol from inside her jacket and aimed it at me.

"Look down the beach," I said. "See those cars coming? How far do you think you're going to get on a golf cart?"

"Barbara, get the fucking money." Dorn yelled.

Wilcox took a step toward me and I flung the money bag into the ocean.

"Fuck!" Wilcox yelled.

"Go get it!" Dorn said.

Barbara ran into the water.

Dorn looked at me. "I'm gonna fucking kill you," he said. "No matter what else happens, I'm gonna fucking kill you."

Up close, Dorn was frightening to look at. His size was twice that of a normal man. His neck alone was over twenty inches, his chest had to be around sixty.

Out of the corner of my eye, I saw Wilcox fighting with the waves, trying to grab the money bag.

Dorn's eyes went wide, the veins in his neck bulged and he charged me like an enraged bull after a cape.

Bo Dorn was not a man to fight fair. He didn't want to beat you so much as murder you and when it was life and death, rules went out the window and survival became priority one.

As he charged me, I spun to my right and kicked his legs out from under him with my left foot.

He hit the sand face first. I didn't give him the chance to get up. I couldn't. I kicked him in the face three times and then in the chest and stomach.

Dorn screamed, not in pain but out of anger.

I kicked him five or six more times. I heard his nose break. Blood ran down his face and neck.

I glanced to my right. Two cars were racing toward us.

Dorn rolled over and got to one knee. I stepped back and reached into my pocket for the heavy set of brass knuckles I tucked away. I slipped them onto my right hand.

Dorn, incredibly, started to stand up.

I waited and timed the punch and then let loose with a right hook. The sound of brass knuckles hitting Dorn's jaw was sickening, yet he didn't go down.

I timed another punch and when the brass knuckles made contact with his jaw, the force lifted him off his feet and he dropped unconscious to the sand.

Lawrence and Walt were just seconds away. "Give it up," I said to Wilcox.

She had the money bag and ran out of the water. "You motherfucker," she yelled at me, "I'll kill you!"

Walt shot her one second before she could shoot me.

Lawrence stood over Dorn with handcuffs. "Jesus Christ, Jack," he said.

Walt knelt beside Wilcox. "She's dead," he said.

"Too bad she didn't read the end of the Fan Dancer, it might have saved her life," I said.

"Yeah," Walt said.

I used my cell phone to call Wally.

"Mr. Bekker, Sheriff Jane is here," Wally said. "Is it okay to stop for something to eat on the way back?"

"I don't see why not," I said.

"We'll be at the IHOP," Wally said.

I hung up and looked at Waly and Lawrence.

"They'll be at the IHOP," I said.

# Chapter Fifty-seven

Wally shook my hand and then hugged Regan and Jane.
"You take care, Wally," Oz said.

Wally shook Oz's hand. "Thank you for putting up with me," Wally said.

Oz nodded to me. "I put up with him, I can put up with anything."

"The money is with the pilots," I said. "Robert will pick you up at the airport."

Wally misted up a bit. "I don't know what to say," he said.

"Then get your ass on the plane and say nothing," Oz said.

We waited until the plane was in the air before we left the airfield.

"I have to go to work," Jane said.

"Me too," Regan said.

"Oz?" I said.

"I ain't had to go to work in fifteen years," Oz said.

"Good. I'll buy you breakfast," I said.

"Good. I'll let you," Oz said.

*   *   *

After lunch, Oz went to his room to take a nap. I changed into sweats and went to the backyard for a workout. My right hand was pretty sore so I stayed away from bag work and concentrated on the weights.

Afterward, I went for a run on the streets. I didn't want to see the beach for a while. I set my watch and jogged for an hour and when I returned home, a white SUV was parked in the driveway.

Oz was standing in the driveway, waiting for me.

"What?" I said.

"Your ex is here," Oz said.

"My ex?" I said.

"Janet," Oz said. "She say she left Clayton, that it was a mistake to marry him. She say she wants you back and will do anything."

"I'll have a talk with her," I said.

"Jane on the way for dinner," Oz said. "She be here in fifteen minutes."

I walked to my car.

"Where you going?" Oz said.

"The Crist mansion," I said. "I'll be back when it's safe."

"Nice knowin' ya," Oz said.

# About the Author

**A**l **Lamanda** is a native of New York City. In addition to his many mysteries, he also writes Western novels under the pen name Ethan J. Wolfe. He has been nominated for many awards, and won the Nero Wolfe Award for Best Mystery of the Year for his novel, *With 6 You Get Wally*, book five in the John Bekker Mysteries. The series continues with *Who Killed Joe Italiano?* (Encircle Publications, 2018), and *For Better or Worse* (Encircle Publications, 2019). His latest stand-alone novel, *City of Darkness*, was published by Encircle in January, 2021, and the first book in his new series, the Rollie Finch Mysteries, entitled *Once Upon a Time on 9/11*, came out in April, 2021. Book two, *Rollie and the Missing Six*, will be published in August of 2022. Al is always working on his next novel.

If you enjoyed reading this book,
please consider writing your honest review
and sharing it with other readers.

Many of our Authors are happy to participate in
Book Club and Reader Group discussions.
For more information, contact us at info@encirclepub.com.

Thank you,
Encircle Publications

For news about more exciting new fiction, join us at:

Facebook: www.facebook.com/encirclepub

Twitter: twitter.com/encirclepub

Instagram: www.instagram.com/encirclepublications

Sign up for Encircle Publications newsletter and specials:
eepurl.com/cs8taP

CPSIA information can be obtained
at www.ICGtesting.com
Printed in the USA
LVHW030259170322
713568LV00004B/328